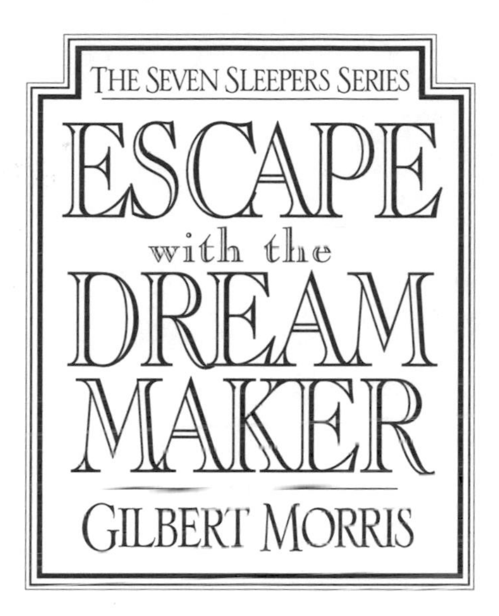

Moody Press
CHICAGO

ISBN: 0-8024-3692-7

3 5 7 9 10 8 6 4 2

Printed in the United States of America

To April Meeks—
the world needs more
sweet, gentle young ladies like you!

Contents

1

Last Days for Nuworld

"I'm so tired, I don't think I can make it another day, Sarah!"

Josh Adams slumped down beside the small stream that wound through the village and locked his fingers behind his head. Josh was a tall, gangling teenager with a mop of auburn hair and dark blue eyes. He closed his eyes, saying, "It seems like it's nothing but one mission after another—and *nothing* ever really gets accomplished."

Sarah Collingwood sat beside him and crossed her legs Indian fashion. She was wearing a pair of faded blue slacks and a man's white shirt. Her black hair had just a trace of red in it. She had large brown eyes and was, at fifteen, experiencing that first bloom of womanhood that comes to young girls. She was small and graceful, but fatigue marked her face as she answered quietly, "I know what you mean, Josh. It's hard to get up every morning knowing that nothing is really going to change."

Five yards away a flock of sparrows began a miniature war, fighting and rolling in the dust. They cheeped angrily, and finally the largest bird appeared to win some sort of victory.

Josh had opened his eyes slightly to watch the battle, and a cynical smile tugged the corners of his lips upward. "You'd think birds could agree, wouldn't you? Even the birds can't get along in this blasted Nuworld!"

"Oldworld wasn't a paradise either," Sarah reminded him. "Birds fought there sometimes too."

But Oldworld was long gone. It had been called Earth once, but a nuclear holocaust had seared the planet. Continents moved, ice caps melted, new lands rose out of the sea. The inhabitants of the world changed too. The explosion caused mutants of all sorts to spring up in the races that developed after the Great Burning. There were giants, and dwarfs, and Snakepeople, and all sorts of alien life forms roaming the planet that was now called Nuworld.

Josh and six other teenagers had been saved from the nuclear explosion by a small group of scientists, including Josh's father. The seven young people had been put into special capsules, where they slept for many years. Finally they had emerged to find a strange planet in which a sinister being called the Dark Lord was engaged in a horrifying struggle against Goél, the leader of the free peoples. The Seven Sleepers, as they were called, became the servants of Goél. He sent them on several dangerous missions, which had taken them under the sea, across burning deserts, to the tops of mountains, and into jungles harboring saber-toothed tigers.

"How much longer do you think it will be?" Sarah asked idly. She plucked a dry dandelion out of the green grass, examined it, blew at it. As the tiny fragments scattered, she tossed the stem down, saying, "I wish we would have done with it. I know Goél is going to win—but sometimes it doesn't *look* like it."

Josh was almost asleep. He mumbled drowsily, "It's not just the physical stuff that's so hard. That's bad enough. I get tired, but I'm tired *inside*. You know what I mean, Sarah?"

"I know. I think they called it 'battle fatigue' back

in the wars on Oldworld. Men just got so tired fighting they couldn't go on."

The two rested, saying little, for in truth they were exhausted. They had actually been little more than children when they had first been called from their sleep capsules; now, Josh and Sarah were sixteen and fifteen and had matured greatly. They had paid a price, however. The strain had taken its toll on them.

Finally they wandered up to the house where the Sleepers had been staying since their last assignment.

Josh looked up the four steps that led to the main floor and shook his head. "I don't know if I can climb those steps," he groaned.

"Sure you can." Sarah took his arm. "Let me help you. I was always taught to respect my elders."

Josh managed a grin. "I'm only a year older than you are." As they reached the landing, he said, "That means we'll never get married."

Sarah shot him a startled look. "What do you mean by that?"

"I've decided to marry an older woman. Maybe someone seventeen."

"I hope you marry a widow who's forty years old and has six redheaded, mean children!"

They stepped inside as Sarah said this, and the five young people who were sprawled around the room heard her comment.

"What do you mean, 'redheaded children'?" Jake Garfield piped up. "Redheaded kids aren't mean. They're like me—easy to get along with." Jake had a New York City accent even after being away for so long. He was small, with brown eyes—and red hair.

A laugh went around the group, and the tallest boy, a handsome, athletic seventeen-year-old named Dave Cooper, added, "Everybody knows redheads are hot-tempered. Now you take us guys with yellow hair and blue eyes—we're right out of *GQ* magazine."

A groan went up, and the girl sitting next to Dave, Abbey Roberts, said, "There's no chance of you winning the humility award, Dave Cooper!"

At fifteen, Abbey had large blue eyes, long blonde hair, and beautifully shaped features. And despite the hardships of their journey, she had managed to dress in a neat light-green skirt and a tan blouse that fit well. She was carefully made up, and her hair was done expertly. She looked over at the small black boy sitting by the window, looking out. "Wash, do *you* think redheads are mean?"

Wash was really named Gregory Randolph Washington Jones. He had been born in New Orleans and had grown up on the street there until he had been popped into a sleep capsule. At fourteen, he was slightly undersized, but he continually wore a cheerful smile. "I suppose redheads are just about like the rest of us. Some good and some bad—but Jake there, I expect he's one of the better redheads."

The young man leaning against the wall beside Wash was six feet one, even though he was only sixteen. Lean, lanky, and muscular, he had very light blue eyes, bleached yellow hair, and was sunburned. Freckles were scattered over his face. His name was Bob Lee Jackson, but everyone called him Reb. He was a true Southerner from the hills of Arkansas originally, who was still fighting the Civil War.

"When do you think we might get out of this place and do something?" Reb asked. "I'm gonna go crazy! It's like being in the pokey. Why, my Uncle Seedy, if he was here, he'd get us on our way toward a new adventure."

A groan went up. Of all the Sleepers, Reb was the only one who continually looked for new adventures.

"Don't tell me about your Uncle Seedy. I don't want to hear about him anymore," Jake protested. He had been busily working on some invention.

"What're you making now?" Josh inquired, coming over to look at the mass of wires and tubes and coils.

Jake stared at him adamantly. "I'm not going to tell you until it's finished. I've taken enough ribbing from you about my inventions."

"I hope it's not a bomb that's going to blow us all up," Sarah said wearily. Then she slumped down onto one of the straight-back chairs. "Though I don't know but what that might be a welcome relief."

"I'm surprised to hear you say so, my daughter." The new voice seemed to come from nowhere.

And then every one of the young people leaped to his feet.

Standing in the doorway was a tall man wearing a light gray robe. He had pushed back the hood, and his long brown hair hung down past his shoulders. He had warm brown eyes, a generous mouth, and could have been anywhere between twenty-five and fifty.

"Goél!" Josh shouted, and instantly his fatigue seemed to drop away. "We've been waiting for you."

"I know you have," Goél said, "but I have had many miles to travel."

"Here, we have some apple cider. Let me heat it up for you, Goél," Sarah said quickly. She was given to touches like that—cooking and keeping house, whenever the Sleepers had a house to keep.

Abbey could not cook an egg without ruining it, but she was good at serving, and as soon as Sarah poured the cider, Abbey served Goél first and then the rest of them. "I hope you like it, sire," she said.

"I'm sure I will," Goél said. He drank gratefully, then took a seat on the chair that Wash had brought.

"Thank you, my son." Goél waved an arm. "All of you sit down. I have many things to say."

"Will you stay long this time, Goél?"

"No, I must be gone almost immediately." When a slight groan went up, a smile touched his full lips. "Some day it will be different, but for now we must do what we must."

Reb said, "Well, that's what John Wayne always said. You all remember? In about a hundred movies he said, 'A man does what he's got to do.' I guess him and you are right, Goél. So what're we going to do now?"

"I know what you would *like* to do." Goél fixed his eyes on the tall boy. "You would like to go back to Camelot, and put on a suit of armor, and fight dragons again."

Reb looked down at the floor, embarrassed. In truth, their adventure to the land of Camelot had been the high point of his life. He had become an expert jouster and had, indeed, done battle with something like a dragon. When he looked up, his light blue eyes glowed. "Is that where we're going? Back to Camelot?"

"I'm afraid not, Reb." Goél seemed to note the disappointment on the young man's face and said, "Few of us get to do just what we'd like to do. That is a prize that must be won. But I promise you that some day, if you trust me and obey, you will come through to your heart's desire."

He then looked around at the Sleepers, and when Goél's eyes locked onto his, Josh thought, *He knows everything I'm thinking—he knows everything I've ever done!* As the eyes continued to hold his, another startling thought came, *And I think he knows everything I'm going to do!* It was disconcerting. Josh, like every other boy and every girl, had a secret life that he would not care to see paraded before everyone's gaze.

Yet, somehow it was comforting to know that here was one who knew all about him but still had faith in him and love for him.

"I'm ready to go wherever you say, Goél," he said simply.

"You are a good servant of Goél, Joshua." There was pleasure in the tall man's eyes. He sipped his cider and for some time sat talking about the groups all over the world that bore his name. They were called, collectively, "The House of Goél," and they comprised all sorts of strange beings as well as those who looked much like dwellers of Oldworld.

Despite Goél's statement that he must leave soon, he found time to speak with each one of the Sleepers alone.

Sarah prepared a fine supper—including steaks and fried potatoes and a salad—and Reb somewhere had found a quantity of fresh milk. They enjoyed the meal together, and afterward, when night came on, Josh lit the lamps.

Finally, Goél arose. "You have a mission to perform once again, and you have never failed me. You have gone through dark hours, dangerous times, but this, I think, will be perhaps your most dangerous mission of all."

"It can't be worse than those giant squid!" Wash exclaimed. It had been Wash who braved an enormous octopuslike creature in the undersea world.

"There may be physical dangers, yes, but some dangers are worse. There are many men and women and young people who could face a physical trial but who would falter before other kinds."

"What other kinds of trials do you mean, Goél?" Sarah asked.

"Spiritual trials are always harder than any other

kind," he said. "We're in a spiritual battle for the world, as well as a physical one, and I would warn each of you to be on guard. You're all my servants, and I'm proud of each one of you. You all have your strengths . . ." His eyes glided again over each one of them as he said quietly, "And you all have your weaknesses. That is the way of men, and it always will be in this world."

"Can you tell us more about the mission, sire?" Dave asked.

"Something strange and terrible has been happening in Nuworld." Goél's face darkened, his eyes smoldered. "Some of my most trusted servants have disappeared."

"*Disappeared!*" Jake exclaimed. "What do you mean?"

"I mean exactly that. They have fallen out of sight." He hesitated, then said, "I caution you again. Be *very* careful! You might be one of the next to disappear. Those that have been taken have been some of my most trusted aides, even as you are."

"But what are we to *do?*" Abbey asked with some bewilderment.

"Your mission is simply to find my servants and bring them back. They have somehow fallen under the power of the Dark Lord, and they must be rescued."

"But how can we find them?"

"That is part of your mission—finding where they have gone. I will give you a helper along the way. But there will be those who would lead you astray. So be very careful."

"How will we know our helper?"

Goél said quietly, "I have given the one who will help you a special phrase. When he meets you, he will say, 'The stars are doing their great dance.' Do not trust anyone who does not say *exactly* those words—'The stars are doing their great dance'—and then you must say as a countersign, 'Yes, and every tree will sing.'"

For a few moments he gave them further instructions, concluding, "As you trust in me, so will your mission succeed. Farewell, my Seven Sleepers." He hesitated, then said, "The last days are upon this planet. The final battle looms on the horizon. I think this may be your last mission before that battle—and your most dangerous. Take care. Remember the signs."

Goél turned and without another word stepped out of the doorway and faded into the darkness.

A silence fell over the group, and at last Josh said wearily, "So we've got to find the missing members of the House of Goél, and then we've got to get them free." He slouched down in his chair, saying nothing more.

As Sarah and Wash began cleaning up the supper dishes, Wash said, "I never seen Josh look so worn out. It looks like he can hardly keep his eyes open."

Sarah glanced over at Josh, who was sprawled in his chair, his head tilted back. "He's exhausted—but then we all are."

"Well, we better get some more get up and go." Then Wash looked down at the dishes in his hands and shook his head. "But it seems like my get up and go done got up and went!"

2

An Odd Sort of Town

For several days the Sleepers spent a great deal of time trying to figure out their strategy. Goél had told them little enough about the crisis; however, he had left a list of his servants who had disappeared.

At their first planning meeting, Josh said, "This list is about all we have to go on. *Something* in this list has to give us some kind of clue. Everyone take a copy and study it. Try to find something on the list that'll help pinpoint how to start."

As simple as the plan sounded, it did not prove to be easy. Each Sleeper studied the names and descriptions of the missing servants. From time to time, they came together to share their findings. The difficulty was that there *were* no findings.

One afternoon they sat around the room, staring at their lists blankly, all of them drained mentally. It was Jake who finally noticed something common to most of the names. He said slowly, "I do see one thing."

"Well, what is it?" Dave demanded. "Anything is better than *nothing.*"

Jake held up his list. "Almost all of these people disappeared from the same general area. Look—I've drawn a map. Every X you see is where they've disappeared."

The Sleepers huddled around Jake, staring down at his map, which he placed flat on the pine table. There was a moment's silence.

Then Wash said, "See how many of them are clustered around that one little spot. What's that town there on the map, Jake?"

"It's called Acton."

"I've heard of it, but I don't guess none of us have ever been there."

Jake said, "It's kind of a gathering place for scientists—inventors and people like that."

"Well, I guess we'd better get over there," Josh said. "I think we'll all go crazy just sitting around here looking at each other and staring at pieces of paper."

They made preparations at once, gathering together clothing, weapons, some food. Traveling in Nuworld was not like travel in Oldworld. There were no trains, no airlines, no Greyhound buses. By foot or by horseback or by sailing ship was all there was. Travel was dangerous too, for the land was full of marauding outlaws. Even worse, the members of a group called the Sanhedrin had vowed to execute the Seven Sleepers. They were under the command of the Dark Lord, and Elmas, his Chief Sorcerer, had made finding the Sleepers his highest priority.

It took several days of winding through the forest and staying off the main roads before the Sleepers finally reached the small town.

"That's it," Josh said, "according to the map. So I think we better split up here."

"Split up? Why should we do that?" Abbey asked. She was wearing a cranberry-colored skirt and a bolero jacket over a light blue blouse. She looked rather fetching, as she always did. "I don't want us to split up. Let's stay together."

"No, that won't do," Josh said. "The servants of the Dark Lord are looking for the *Seven* Sleepers. What we need to do is go into town one at a time and find places to stay. Elmas will have his spies there, and if he hears of seven young people coming in together, we'll be caught for sure."

"I think that's smart," Reb said. "Old Stonewall Jackson himself couldn't have figured out a better battle plan than that." He smiled. "But how are we going to talk to each other?"

They spent some time figuring out a communication system. Since they would be separated, never to be seen together, one Sleeper would communicate with another, who would pass along the message until all were aware.

"It sounds awkward to me." Dave shook his head. "What if we have to get together in a hurry?"

"We'll have to figure that out when it happens," Josh said rather sharply. "No plan's perfect. We'll just have to play it by ear."

They followed Josh's plan, some of them staying outside Acton for a day or two. None went in from the same road.

Josh, who had remained outside until last, chose to come in from the east. Entering Acton, he noticed at once that it was larger and more sophisticated than most other towns in Nuworld. He had disguised himself somewhat, putting on the clothes of a peasant, and he tried to appear as country as possible. If anyone asked, he was a yokel come to seek work in the city. He'd put dirt on his face, and he thought he looked properly disreputable.

He approached an inn, entered, and saw that it was almost empty. Two old men sat playing chess and taking sips from flagons that rested on the table.

The innkeeper was a dark-skinned burly man with a fierce head of black hair. He had quick, sharp black eyes. "What'll it be?" he asked, then demanded, "You're a stranger here?"

"Yes, I am. I come to town lookin' for work." Josh slurred his speech. "You know where a man might get work?"

"Not for the likes of you," the innkeeper sniffed.

"Well, could I get a place to stay?"

The innkeeper hesitated. "I've got a room out back over the stable. It's not much but probably all you'll be able to afford."

Josh asked to see the place, and it proved to be rough indeed. However, it was all he needed. He paid the innkeeper a week's rent and then asked, "Could I buy a meal?"

At the sight of money, the innkeeper had perked up. "I'll have the wife put on a steak. Come in and have a drink on the house."

Josh went back inside and sat down. The innkeeper, having a paying customer, grew more talkative.

"Business seems pretty slow," Josh said as he sipped at the powerful drink that filled his cup. He had to at least make a show of drinking it, and he smacked his lips as though it were delicious.

"Aye, times are a little odd." The innkeeper shook his head dolefully. "I been running this inn since I was a young man. Never seen times like this. Seems like nobody wants to get out at night anymore." He looked around at the two old men and shrugged. "Up until a while back, the place would be full every night. People come to drink and have a good time. Not no more, though."

"Where are they?"

"Can't say."

The answer was sharp, and Josh felt a sudden resistance in the man. He did not want him to become suspicious, so he asked no more questions.

After the meal, however, Josh wandered out

through the town and tried to make other contacts. Once he passed Sarah, who did not even look at him. He avoided her gaze, too, and passed without speaking. *Going to be hard to do,* he thought, *ignoring Sarah and the others like that, but it's the safest thing to do.*

Josh discovered little on that first foray, and he went back to his room, planning to try to find out more the next day.

The next day, however, proved to be frustrating as well. He stopped at a leather shop to get a tear in one of his boots sewed up. The cobbler accepted the boot, looked at it, and said, "Aye, I can fix it."

Josh sat down and watched him work slowly and methodically on the boot. From time to time, the man would glance at a clock that was on the wall.

Josh began to speak idly, admitting he was a stranger in town. He tried to pump the cobbler for details of one of the missing people, a woman named Jewel.

"Aye, she was here, but she's gone now. I haven't seen her. Don't know where she went."

Something about the man's manner of speaking caught at Josh. His speech was somehow . . . well . . . *mechanical* was the only word Josh could come up with. It was as if the cobbler's mind was far away, and when he finally came back he did not speak much.

When the shoemaker finished the boot and named the price, Josh looked into his eyes. He saw that there was something odd about them. Not their shape, for the cobbler was not a bad-looking fellow—not more than thirty, fair hair, blue eyes. It was the *expression* in the eyes that puzzled Josh. *It's almost like there's nobody home,* he thought, and even he did not know what he meant by that.

"Not much going on in town is there?"

"About like usual, I guess."

"What does a fellow do here for excitement?"

The cobbler stared at him as if he had not heard, then turned away and started working on a belt.

Everywhere Josh went that day, that sort of thing happened.

Bewildered, he went back to the inn, where he ate supper. No more than half a dozen people were there that night, and most of them were old. Finally, he went to bed, wearily thinking, *We've got to do better than this. I'll contact the others tomorrow and see if any of them has found out anything.*

The next day he met Sarah by prearrangement in a market where a few vendors sold their wares. The two of them seemed to meet by accident and managed to find their way to a deserted section down a side street.

"I don't think anybody's watching us," Josh said. "What have you found out?"

"Not a thing, Josh," she said.

"You've got to have found out *something.*"

"Well, what about you?" Sarah exclaimed. Acting hurt by Josh's tone, she said, "You've had as much chance to look around as I've had."

Josh was irritable and allowed himself to speak back sharply. Soon the two were arguing. Their voices rose, and a man walking by looked at them curiously.

Instantly Josh and Sarah turned and walked away. "Well, that was dumb," Josh said. "We've got to find a place to meet where nobody can see us."

"I don't think it matters, Josh," Sarah said. "I don't think we're going to find anything here."

"We've got to find something. This place is the only clue we have. Have you talked to any of the others?"

"Yes, I talked to Dave. He's pretending to be a merchant, stopping for a few days in town. He hasn't found out anything either, and he said he talked to Jake, and Jake didn't know anything."

The two walked on silently until Josh abruptly said, "It looks hopeless, Sarah."

"What about the man that's supposed to help us?"

"There's no way for us to find him." Josh shrugged. "We'll have to wait for him to come to us. I guess that's all we can do now—just wait."

Sarah stared at Josh oddly. "You're not yourself, Josh."

"What's that supposed to mean?"

"I mean you're not acting like your old self." Sarah seemed to find it difficult to explain. "I know you're tired, but all of us are."

"Well, we can get rested up here. Nothing to do but wait," Josh said moodily. He kicked at a stone and sent it flying. "I always did hate to wait. I won't get in a line if there's any way to stay out of it. My folks always said I was too impatient."

"Your dad didn't think so."

Sarah had lived with Josh's family for a time before the Great Burning. It was one thing that tied them together. Josh loved to hear Sarah talk about his parents. They were his tie, in his memory, to his old life.

"I wish Dad were here," Josh said. "He'd know how to handle this."

It was a futile wish, and Josh knew it. His father had helped them out of the sleep capsules and then had died.

Sarah took his arm, and he turned to face her. "I'm sorry. I didn't mean to be critical, Josh," she said softly. "I know this is getting to all of us, but Goél said it won't be long now. The last battle is coming—very soon."

"I wish it was here today!" Josh frowned. "Tell the others to get word to me at once if Goél's servant contacts them. We've got to do something soon. Good-bye, Sarah."

Sarah watched Josh walk off. *He isn't going to last like this*, she said to herself. *I've never seen him so nervous and upset. We've got to do something!*

3
Oliver

For five days Josh felt his nerves getting more and more ragged. Every morning he arose, went out on the streets of Acton, visited stores, shops, talked to the people on the streets—such as would listen.

But absolutely nothing happened. In one meeting with Sarah, he complained, "These people are closer than clams. They don't talk about anything except the weather."

Sarah had been equally disappointed. "It's like they're here—but they're not here," she said. "I try to talk to them, and they answer back, but they never really *say* anything, if you know what I mean. They seem to be going through the motions. Their minds are someplace else. And at night there's nothing doing. It's sort of like a ghost town."

Josh had noted this also, and it puzzled him. He had considered leaving Acton and striking out cross-country in hope of finding Goél—but in the first place, he didn't know where Goél was. He did know that Goél had entrusted them with this mission, and there seemed nothing better to do than to stay.

As the days passed, he grew more weary. From time to time, he would see one of the other Sleepers, but they all carefully ignored each other.

One morning Josh woke up feeling terrible. It was like he was coming down with the flu, although he knew the problem was more a mental thing. Getting out of bed slowly, he moved like an old man. He pulled his clothes on, stared at himself in the mirror, and decided to skip brushing his hair or washing his face. "What difference does it make?" he said aloud to his image. "Nobody's going to pay any attention to me anyway. It's like living with a bunch of zombies."

He passed through the inn and did not even stop to eat breakfast. He had lost his appetite and sometimes would forget several meals in a row. He could tell he was losing weight from the way his clothes were beginning to hang on him, but even this did not seem to be important.

All morning Josh walked around the town, slowly, stopping from time to time to sit on a bench in front of a shop. He had stopped striking up conversations, for that seemed futile. All that was left to do was to wait—and he was not good at waiting.

When the sun was high overhead, he felt thirsty and walked toward a pump that was set in the middle of the street. There was a tin cup attached. He pumped up some of the water and found it had a harsh, metallic taste. He swallowed a couple of mouthfuls and spit the rest out.

"That's the worst water I've ever tasted."

Josh turned quickly. The voice had been cheerful, unlike the voices of most citizens of Acton. He found himself staring at a man of about fifty with a pair of steady gray eyes and a Van Dyke beard. He was wearing khakis and was neat and wiry.

"Yes, it is bad," Josh said.

"I was just going into that inn over there to have something a little better than this water. Care to join me?"

"Why—I don't mind if I do."

"Come along, then. By the way, my name's Oliver."

"I'm Josh." It had been a little risky to use his real

name, but Josh had chosen to do so. If he took a name such as *Tom* and someone called for Tom, he knew he would ignore it.

Walking alongside the newcomer, Josh felt a flash of hope. Here was the first person he had met in Acton who seemed to be alert and open to conversation.

"Well, innkeeper, let's have some of your best cider," Oliver said. "Bring us a whole jug. I'm dry as dust."

"Yes, sir!"

When the innkeeper brought the jug, Oliver paid him and picked up the two glasses. "Let's sit outside at that table. I like fresh air."

"So do I." Josh followed the man outside, the two sat down, and he watched Oliver fill the glasses. Picking his up, he tasted it and said, "This is good."

"Yes, it is, isn't it? Are you a stranger here?"

"Yes, just came in from the country, looking for work."

"Not much work going on in Acton."

"So I've found out. Haven't been able to find anything."

Oliver spoke with some assurance of the countryside. He informed Josh that there was not a great deal of work around Acton, except for someone who had a trade. He seemed relaxed as he sat there, and he talked generally about the town, about the crops, and about what was happening in the world. He seemed to be well informed.

Suddenly Oliver looked directly at Josh and said clearly, "The stars are doing their great dance."

Instantly Josh felt a thrill of recognition. *The password!* He gave the response, "Yes, and every tree will sing."

Oliver laughed out loud, then put his hand out. He

grasped Josh's with surprising strength. "That's some disguise you have on there, Josh."

"Well, it's about all I could come up with." Josh began to talk eagerly. "I'd about given up on finding you, Oliver. Have you been here all the time?"

"I'm in and out. I have to make a living, you know."

"Have you made any headway on finding out where the missing servants of Goél have gone?"

"Not really, but we'll find them. Where is the rest of your group?"

"They're here in Acton. We thought it better not to come in together."

Oliver nodded approvingly. "Very wise. The Sanhedrin would have spotted seven young visitors instantly. Let's think of some way that you and I can be together while we're figuring out how to go about our problem."

"How could we do that?"

"Oh, I've got a little money. Suppose I hire you to do some work for me?"

"What kind of work do you do, Oliver?"

"I'm a scientist."

"Really? My father was a scientist."

"You look like a bright young fellow. You probably have some science in you."

"No, not very much, I'm afraid," Josh said ruefully. "I guess I take after my mother."

"That's probably just as well. Actually, I'm an inventor. Most of my inventions don't work, however." He laughed cheerfully at his own remark. "They all work except for one little flaw, which makes them useless," he added.

"What are you working on now?"

"I've found something that I think could be quite potent. It's not fully developed yet, but it's quite an invention, if I do say so myself." His eyes glowed, and he leaned back, sipping the cider. "Yes," he said, "I could hire you, and that way we can spend a great deal of time together without looking suspicious. Let everybody know that you are working for me."

"That sounds good to me. Tell me more about your invention."

Oliver leaned forward, and his gray eyes gleamed. "I'm working on something really big, Josh. If it works—" He broke off and laughed at himself again. "I sound like every wild-eyed inventor in the world, don't I?" Then he sobered and said, "But if it works, Josh, it'll change the whole world as we know it."

"Can't you tell me about it?"

"Oh, no. Not good luck to talk about things like that things you're going to do. But I can tell you about my *smaller* invention."

"All right, let's hear it."

"Well, back in Oldworld they had things called television."

"Why, of course, I remember that. We had a television."

Oliver blinked with surprise. "Of course. I forgot you came from Oldworld in the sleep capsules. As you know, there hasn't been anything like television for a long time—most technology was wiped out. I'd like to hear about television. I never actually saw one. Tell me about it."

Josh told about television and about some of the programs that he had liked.

Oliver listened carefully. When Josh ended, he said, "Well, if you can imagine a combination book, television, and docudrama, that would be sort of what my invention is like."

"I don't understand."

"Come along. I'll give you a demonstration. We'll

take the rest of this cider with us."

Ten minutes later Josh was inside a large room in a house on the outskirts of town. The room was filled with all sorts of equipment, wires, and blinking bulbs, all of it incomprehensible to him. "Jake would love this," he said. "He's quite an inventor himself."

"Is he now? Perhaps we can use him." Oliver smiled. "Come over here, and I'll give you a quick demonstration."

Josh stepped to the chair that Oliver motioned him to and sat down at his command.

Oliver picked up something that looked like headphones, except that it had rods instead of earpieces.

"This fits over the head, you see? We'll take it very easy."

Josh sat there as Oliver put the headpiece over his head. He noticed that the wires ran to a complicated-looking black machine.

Seeing his eyes, Oliver said, "That's what does the work, right there."

"How does it work?"

Oliver adjusted the headset, then snapped his fingers. "Oh, yes, I found out this helps." He went over to a cabinet mounted on the wall, took out a bottle of clear liquid, and poured a few drops into a glass of cider. "Here." Stirring it with a wooden spoon, he handed it to Josh. "Just sip some of that."

"What is it?"

"Actually it makes your mind very active, but you probably won't feel a thing. It helps with the Dream Maker."

"Is that what this is called? The Dream Maker?" Josh sniffed at the contents of the glass, then drank it down. It seemed to have no effect, and he said, "How does the machine work?"

Oliver sat in front of him. His eyes were bright as he explained his invention. "The Dream Maker, as I told you, Josh, is somewhat like television, but it's like being *in* a play instead of just watching. The box there is like a computer. It has all sorts of things in it on disk. Books, for example. Did you ever read a book called *A Tale of Two Cities?"*

"Why, yes. That's by Dickens. I've read that book."

"Well, it's on the hard drive there. So you've got the book there, you've got your mind here, and the innervision takes the information—the book, that is—and you become a part of it. It's like you're in the book itself. Like you're in a dramatized, television version of the book. For example, if I set these dials, suddenly you're living in *A Tale of Two Cities."*

Josh listened closely, and it all sounded fantastic. Oliver's eyes appeared even brighter, and the drink seemed to have made him a little sleepy. He asked a few questions, and then Oliver said, "Would you like a sample?"

"Why, sure. Can I go to the last part of the book where Sydney Carton dies on the scaffold?"

"I don't see why not," Oliver said cheerfully. "Sit there and concentrate on me while I set the dials."

Josh never knew exactly how it happened. He just watched Oliver for a moment as he turned certain dials and pushed certain buttons.

Then Oliver said, "Now, think about *A Tale of Two Cities*. Think about Sydney Carton."

Suddenly Josh found himself drifting away. His vision was becoming blurred. He could still see Oliver's bright gray eyes, and he could hear Oliver speaking, but it was as if he were far away.

And then it happened!

"Make way for the cart. Look, 'e won't be keeping that head long, will 'e now?"

Josh was walking alongside a cart pulled by two gray horses. Inside the cart was a prisoner. He had a pale face but did not look like a man who was worried. He was wearing a dark gray suit with a frilly shirt collar, and he appeared not to hear those who were yelling at him from the streets.

Josh found himself jostled by the people who were accompanying the cart. Most of them were wearing baggy trousers, and many of them had rags tied around their heads. They were speaking French, and Josh discovered that he could speak French as well.

Somebody nudged him, "Who is that in there?"

Josh said at once, "Sydney Carton."

"No, that ain't his name. It's something else," the Frenchman said.

Josh edged closer to the cart.

The condemned man looked at him and smiled.

Josh said in French, "Can I get you away? I'll help you make your escape."

"No, my boy. That's a kind thought. You're not one of these, even though you're dressed like them."

Josh looked down to see that he himself was wearing baggy breeches. He saw that his hands were tanned very brown. Still he was Josh Adams—but somehow on the way to the scaffold with Sydney Carton!

It was all just like in the book! The death carts rumbled along the Paris streets. Ridges of faces looked upward as they plowed through the crowds. A guard of horsemen rode abreast of the procession. The crowd made way for them, then came closer to stare at the condemned people who huddled in the wagons.

Josh stumbled along, noting that Sidney Carton was holding the hand of a frightened young woman, perhaps trying to give her courage. A smile was on his face, and he seemed to have no thought at all for the scene about him.

The clocks of the city began to strike three, and then the carts were in front of the guillotine. Before it, seated in chairs, were a number of women, busily knitting. They had come to see the "entertainment," Josh knew, and he despised them!

And then Carton descended from the cart, still holding the hand of the young woman.

Josh heard her say, "But for you, dear stranger, I should not be so composed, for I am naturally a poor little thing, faint of heart; nor should I have been able to raise my thought to Him who was put to death, that we might have hope and comfort here today. I think you were sent to me by heaven."

"Keep your eyes on me, dear child . . ." Sidney Carton said.

"I mind nothing while I hold your hand."

"They will be rapid. Fear not!"

Josh listened as the two spoke quietly, and then the girl asked Carton if he thought she would feel grief in heaven, and if she would miss her dear sister whom she must leave.

"It cannot be, my child; there is no Time there, and no trouble there."

Finally the time of execution came, and Sydney Carton looked out at the crowd, saying, "It is a far, far better thing that I do now than I have ever done. It is a far, far better rest that I go to than I have ever known."

Josh could not bear to see the man die. He turned away and shoved his way through the crowd, but he heard the blade strike the block, and a wild cry went up from the crowd that marked the death of a brave man.

"All right, Josh. Come out of it."

Josh suddenly blinked his eyes, startled. He looked around. There was no death cart, no guillotine, no Sydney Carton—he was back in Oliver's room. Oliver had taken the headpiece and was grinning at him. "Well, now you know what innervision does. How do you like it?"

Josh rubbed his temples. He could still feel the imprint of the headpiece, and it seemed his head was humming a little. He felt sleepy and oddly relaxed.

"Why—it's marvelous!" he said.

"Actually, it's just another form of entertainment. Does make you feel relaxed though, doesn't it?"

Josh discovered that this was indeed true. He felt more relaxed than he had felt in weeks. "It does!" he exclaimed with surprise. "Why, I've never seen anything like it!"

"I guess that's all I need to hear, as an artist and an inventor." Oliver did not seem terribly excited. "As I say, Josh, it's just a small thing. Most of the villagers come in and enjoy it. They like relaxation too, you know."

Josh was still amazed. "But it was so—so *real,*" he whispered. "Oliver, it was just like I was there in the book. Can you do that with other books?"

"Oh, yes. Books—and some old television videos that were left. You could be back with John Wayne in *Red River*, that old cowboy movie. I've got that one, I think."

"Reb would love that!"

"Reb? Oh, one of the other Sleepers. Yes, of course. Well—" Oliver seemed to make little of his wonderful invention "—it *is* rather fun. I go into it myself pretty often. It keeps a man from going crazy with boredom. But we've got to talk about finding those who are lost. Goél is expecting that. I think we'd better have a meeting of all the Sleepers—or one at a time, perhaps. Why don't you send them by here, and let me talk to each of them about our mission? This could be a focal gathering point for the group."

"Do you really think we can find Goél's servants, Oliver?"

"I'm sure we can, Josh. Now then, what shall we do next?"

Josh hesitated. "Could I try the innervision again?"

"Why, nothing simpler. What would you like?"

Josh thought for a moment and said, "Do you have a book on the machine called *The Call of the Wild?*"

"As it happens, I do. It's about the North, isn't it? Wolves, sled dogs, and all of that?"

"Yes."

"Well, just sit right down here." Oliver turned and went to the cabinet again, where he added drops to a fresh glass of cider. "Take that, and you're off running through the frozen North behind a pack of sled dogs. Here you go, Josh . . ."

4

A Fellow Needs a Lift!

The quest for the disappearing members of the House of Goél seemed absolutely hopeless. Two more weeks went by, and not a single clue turned up that led to any discoveries. Josh spent hours every day thinking of some way to get at the problem, but nothing came to mind—nor to any of the other Sleepers.

The most profitable—or at least the most pleasant—times of Josh's life came during those hours that he spent with Oliver. He had gotten very close to the older man, and every night the two would sit and talk. Oliver had led an exciting life, and he kept Josh spell bound with tales of his adventures all over the globe. He was an excellent cook too, so that Josh seemed to be gaining back some of the weight that he had lost. He also felt a great deal calmer.

After they had cooked supper and talked for some time, sooner or later Josh would say, "I'd like to try the Dream Maker again, Oliver. If you don't mind."

"Mind, my boy? Why should I mind?" Oliver would instantly put the headset onto Josh's temples, offer him some of the colorless tranquilizer, usually in a glass of fruit juice, then would inquire as to which dream he would like to have.

Night after night this went on, and Josh learned to quickly allow the machine to take over so that he could plunge almost immediately into whatever book or television series or documentary or movie that he wished.

It seemed that Oliver had almost everything on

tape. Josh experienced sailing with Sir Francis Drake in the fight against the great Spanish Armada; he rode with General Sheridan's cavalry in the Civil War. He even went into some of the Hardy Boys' adventures that he had read over and over again while back in Oldworld.

After these sessions, Josh always noticed that he would feel completely relaxed and slept like a log all night. Once he asked Oliver, "Do you think doing this is dangerous?"

Oliver's eyes opened wide. "Why, of course not, Josh. You don't think I'd subject you to these dreams if they were. After all," he added, putting a hand on Josh's shoulder in kindly fashion, "a fellow needs a lift. You've been under tremendous pressure, and anything that can give you relief from that will be of help to the general cause. After all, you're the leader, and your mind needs to be clear. Don't worry about anything."

Oliver and Josh were sitting around one evening, and the inventor had been talking about the difficulty of their mission. His brow furrowed, and his lips drew tight as he said, "This is a terribly difficult task, and we seem to be getting nowhere. But that's the way it is sometimes."

"You're right," Josh said, "and I don't know how long we can hold out."

"That's the question. I'm getting rather edgy myself."

Josh stared at him with amazement. "Why, you never show the least sign of strain. I envy you, Oliver."

"Well, perhaps I keep it covered better than most. I've learned to do that." Oliver shrugged. He set his gray eyes on Josh and seemed to think hard. "I've been thinking about something, but I've hesitated to mention it."

"What is it?" Josh asked quickly.

"You're the leader—I'm just sent to help you—but have you ever thought that some of the other Sleepers may be in danger?"

"Well, of course, there's always danger of the Sanhedrin finding us."

"No, I don't mean that," Oliver interrupted. "I mean—Josh, when we first met, your nerves were like a fine wire drawn so tight that one touch would make it snap. And now look at you." He smiled broadly and waved a hand at him. "You're calm, you're collected, you think clearly."

"Well, I guess I can thank you for that." Josh looked over at the dream machine. "It helps a lot, these evenings spent with the Dream Maker."

Oliver leaned forward and nodded eagerly. "That's exactly what I mean. *You're* calm—what about the others?"

Josh blinked, then said with some embarrassment, "You know, I never thought about them. You must be right, though. Yes, you *are* right." He stood and walked around the room, running his hand through his hair. "You *are* right," he repeated.

"I don't see any real problem. Why don't you just start sending them by—at different times, of course—and let them enjoy the Dream Maker too?"

"That's a great idea!" Josh smiled. "I don't know why I didn't think of it."

"Oh, you would have in time, I'm sure." Then Oliver slapped his thighs and said, "Well, how would you like to visit, oh, say, Robinson Crusoe on a desert island?"

Josh's eyes gleamed. "I've always loved that book. Won't he be surprised to see me, though? Him and Friday . . ."

Josh met with Sarah secretly a few days later.

"What do you think, Sarah?" He knew from Oliver that she had already visited him twice and had been introduced to the Dream Maker techniques.

"It was so *strange*," she said slowly. "I couldn't believe it at first, but it's actually like being there." Her face had a look of wonder, and she shook her head slightly. "But I just don't know. It's kind of weird!"

"I guess all new inventions are that way. Think how odd television was to people that had never seen one. New things like this always take a little getting used to. But the Dream Maker is better than any book I ever read or than any movie I ever saw. Why, it's more fun than *anything* else."

"I suppose," Sarah said doubtfully, "but you know, a person could get addicted to that thing."

Josh grinned and shrugged his shoulders. "I know—it's just like people became couch potatoes back in Oldworld and sat and watched television all day long. I can see how that could happen, but we'll just have to be careful."

Finally Sarah said, "I think everybody has had at least one experience on the Dream Maker—and they all seemed to like it. Except Wash."

"What about Wash?"

"Oh, I don't know. He was really funny when he came back yesterday. I knew he had been to Oliver's and tried out the Dream Maker, but he wouldn't say much about it. The rest of us were all excited, talking about what we were going to do and where we were going in the future, which books and so forth—but Wash just didn't say much of anything."

Later on, Josh cautiously made his way to the room that Wash occupied. He gave their secret signal, a combination of short and long knocks, and the door opened.

"Come on in, Josh." Wash stepped back, and when Josh had slipped through, he shut the door. "It's good to see you. Here, sit down. I got some fresh cake that I bought from the bakery today."

Josh sat, and the two ate cake and talked.

After the cake was finished, Josh said eagerly, "So what do you think of Oliver's invention?"

"The Dream Maker, he calls it." Wash rolled his eyes. "I just don't know, Josh."

"Well, I think it's great. Everybody else does too. What's wrong with it?"

"Nothing, I guess. It's just not my kind of thing."

"It's just something to relax with. We've got a hard job here, and we don't know how long it will go on."

Wash appeared embarrassed. He was an easygoing young man. He had the greatest respect for Josh Adams. He trusted Josh as the leader—always had. Josh knew all that. But now he seemed hesitant to speak.

"Come on, I can see it's bothering you, but I don't understand why."

"Oh, it's just the way I am, I guess. I always was easy to get hooked on things," Wash said slowly. "Back when I was just a kid I got a trumpet, and I just didn't do anything but play the trumpet for the next two years. I mean, no sports, didn't study for school, flunked out on everything. All I did was play that trumpet."

"But you got good at it. I've heard you."

"I guess so. But that two years—it's kind of taken out of my life. I didn't make any friends. I didn't spend time with my family. They all tried to tell me I was becoming a regular fanatic."

"I don't see that was all that bad."

Wash scratched his nose, then added slowly, "And it wasn't just that. I got into collecting baseball cards, and then comic books, and I'll tell you, Josh, I just seemed to get lost in it. When I was into baseball cards, I couldn't think of anything except gettin' that next card. The same thing with comic books. I'd go to all the shows. And study books about the prices and the rare ones. Even almost got a copy of the first *Superman*. Boy, that would have made me rich! I didn't, though."

"All of us collect things at times when we're kids."

Wash seemed even more embarrassed. "I guess you just don't understand, Josh. You see, somebody told me once that I had an 'addictive personality.' I didn't know what that meant, and he said it meant that I just had to keep on doing whatever I was doing with everything I had."

Josh could not grasp this. "But that's what Olympic athletes do all the time."

"And I'm not even sure *that's* good. It's a real lopsided life. Some of those people work every hour of every day that they can for four years. Maybe they win a gold medal, but what about that four years?"

The two boys talked late into the night. Finally, Josh threw up his hands. "I don't think you're right about this, Wash. I think you need to have some R & R—rest and recreation. All of us do."

Wash smiled. "I guess you're right, Josh. I just don't want to get hooked on that thing like I did on some other things in my life."

"You won't." Josh slapped the younger boy on the shoulder affectionately. "We'll look after each other. If I get hooked, just take a stick and hit me with it, and I'll do the same for you."

"All *righhht!*" Wash made the high-five sign and took Josh's slap.

Then Josh headed for the door.

"Sure been nice talking to you," Wash said. "I'll be glad when this hiding out is over, and we can all be together again."

"It won't be long, I hope. Good night, Wash."

The door closed, and Wash stood there for a long time. He was lonesome in this room. He was a young man who liked company. The isolation had been more difficult for him perhaps than for some of the other Sleepers. Besides, he was the youngest and depended upon the others, especially Reb. The two of them had spent almost no time together recently.

He went to bed, thinking about what Josh had said, and sleepily he muttered, "I'll talk to Reb about it in the morning. I'd like to know how he feels about the Dream Maker."

Reb stared at Wash and shook his head, his lips pursed suddenly. "I think you're all wet, Wash. There's nothing wrong with Dream Maker. Why, I been having the time of my life." His eyes glistened, and he said enthusiastically, "Know what I did? I went back and became a knight in King Arthur's Court! There's some good books about that. Boy, have I ever had fun!"

"I'm glad for that," Wash said. "I just guess maybe I'm the one that needs to watch out."

"Why, you're all right. You're no different from the rest of us."

"Yea, I think I am," Wash said. He tried hard to explain to Reb about what he felt was his character flaw, and finally ended up saying, "I just get hooked on things and go crazy, it seems like. I can't think about anything else."

Reb had become very fond of Wash over the months since they had come to Nuworld. The two had learned to trust one another through long, hard, and dangerous adventures. Now Reb was concerned about his younger friend. He sat listening as Wash tried to explain his problem. Then he said, "That's all right, Wash. I can understand a little about that. I was the same way about cigarettes. I was afraid I'd get hooked on 'em and wouldn't be able to quit."

"That's exactly what I mean," Wash said eagerly. "I know lots of people that started smoking just for fun. They said they could quit anytime they wanted to—but when they tried, they found out somehow they couldn't."

"That's true enough, but I think this is a little bit different. Moderation, that's what you need. Just enough Dream Maker to have a little fun. A fellow needs a break every now and then, you know."

"All right," Wash said. "I'll try it a little bit more." He smiled and said with some embarrassment, "Sorry to be such a wet blanket."

"Aw, you ain't no wet blanket. You'll do to ride with." Reb slapped Wash on the shoulder, and the two turned to talking about earlier times.

As Wash went back to his small room that night, he said, "I guess I'm the one who's out of step. Everybody else thinks this thing's all right. So I guess I'll just have to go along with it."

5
Hooked

Wash and Reb drifted down the street. It was almost dark, and the shadows were long at their feet. All day long they had been busy, for Wash thought he had turned up a lead on one of the missing persons on their list. They had spent all afternoon trying to talk to citizens, but absolutely nothing had come of it.

Wash kicked at a can that lay in his path and sent it winging through the air. It fell to the earth and rattled, then stopped. "We sure wasted a day. I don't know what's wrong with these people," he muttered.

Reb seemed preoccupied. "Huh? What did you say, Wash?"

Wash shot him a quick look. He had noticed that Reb's mind seemed to be elsewhere all through their pursuit of clues. He thought, *Reb's not as quick-minded as he usually is. I wonder if something's bothering him.* Aloud he said, "I just said the people in this town seem like they're all out of it."

"I guess so," Reb said in an offhanded fashion. Then he seemed to forget the conversation and said, "I guess I better get going."

"You going home?"

"No, I'm going by Oliver's. Thought I'd try something a little bit different tonight."

"What's that?" Wash asked.

"Oh, I saw a documentary one time about a gunfight at the OK Corral—back in Dodge City, I think it was. I thought I'd go see what that was like."

“I remember that. It’s pretty violent—you might get shot.”

“Yeah, but it’s just a dream,” Reb quickly answered. “Come along with me. You know there’s a way for two people to dream the same dream?”

Wash looked up with some surprise. “I didn’t know that. How does Oliver do it?”

“Oh, he puts on twin headsets. Then both of us would be at the OK Corral.”

“No, thanks. Include me out,” Wash said. “I don’t want to be around no gun fighting.”

Reb seemed irritated. “Have you ever been back to try the Dream Maker machine out?”

“Well, I been meaning to, but I’ve just been busy.” This was not wholly the truth. Wash had started to go several times but always found some excuse. Now he said defensively, “Maybe I’ll go tomorrow.”

“What would you like to live through again? Some television movie, maybe, or a book?”

Wash had not thought about it at all, but now he said, “I read a book called *Huckleberry Finn* once.”

“Sure, everybody’s read that book. You gonna try it?”

“It might be fun. My favorite part was when Jim and Huck were on the raft, just floating down the river.” Wash’s eyes grew dreamy as they walked along. “Remember old Huck said, ‘There ain’t so much fun or so peaceful as floatin’ down the river.’ I’d sure like to try floating on that raft.”

“Why, sure. That’s what you ought to do. Maybe I’ll come along with you.”

“Hey, that’d be good!” Wash said quickly.

“Or, better still, you come along with me tonight, Wash, and I’ll come with you tomorrow.”

Wash still found the idea of reliving a gunfight

unappealing. "I'm pretty tired. I think I'll go home and go to bed."

"OK," Reb agreed amiably. "I'll see you tomorrow, and we'll float down that river raft with Jim and Huck. Good night, Wash."

"Good night, Reb."

Reb left his friend and made his way to Oliver's house. He knocked, and instantly Oliver's voice called out cheerfully, "Come in!"

"It's good to see you, Reb," the inventor said. "Here, sit down. Tell me what you've been doing."

"Aw, nothing really. Wasting time mostly."

"Oh, I'm not sure about that."

"Yeah, I reckon so. Me and Wash, we hunted all over this town for some trace of a fellow named Bant. Didn't find him though, not even a smell of him. Have no idea where he is, and nobody will talk about it."

"We'll just have to keep on trying. You had supper?"

"Oh, I had a bite." Reb looked anxiously at the Dream Maker. "I got an idea about something I'd like to do."

"What's that?"

"There used to be a TV documentary all about Wyatt Earp facin' down a bunch of mean guys called the Clantons. Doc Holliday was in it too."

"Yes, I have that. Lots of pretty serious action in there. Are you sure you'd like to try it?"

"Sure," Reb said quickly. "If you don't mind going to all that trouble."

"Why, it's no trouble at all. Here, sit down, and we'll get you hooked up."

Reb almost ran to the dream machine. His days were boring, and he lived now for these exciting adventures at night. Secretly he wished he could stay in the Dream Maker chair all the time and dream, but he was afraid to say so. He hid his impatience while Oliver gave him a glass with the colorless liquid in it. He drank it down.

Oliver smiled as he took a seat across from him. "Think about the OK Corral." He moved his dials and then turned and began speaking softly in a singsong voice. "You're going to sleep now, and you're going to wake up in the OK Corral . . ."

The sun was hot, and the gun belt pulled at his thigh. Far ahead to his right, a tall man wearing a raincoat and carrying a shotgun moved steadily ahead. That was Wyatt Earp, Reb knew. To his left walked another man, smaller, carrying a pistol loosely in his left hand. This was Doc Holliday. Morgan, Wyatt's brother, was on the other side.

Suddenly, down the street, Reb caught the flash of movement.

"There they are, boys," Wyatt Earp said. "Be sure you let them start it."

"They'll start it all right," Doc Holliday said grimly. "They're out to get you, Wyatt. Ike Clanton said he'd kill you." He turned to Reb. "You sure that gun's loaded?"

Reb said deep in his throat, "Don't worry about me, Doc. You won't find me behind when the shootin' starts."

"I like a young fella that feels his oats," Doc Holliday said. "Good thing this boy joined us, Wyatt."

Wyatt Earp was a serious-looking man. His reputation as a gunfighter was legendary, and Reb felt a thrill as he looked into the sheriff's gray-blue eyes.

"Glad to have you, Reb, but it's dangerous, you understand."

"I reckon I understand that," Reb said. Then he looked down the street again. "Look, there's Billy Clanton."

Reb advanced with the lawmen, his nerves growing tense. He knew that soon the air would be filled with flying lead, that men would lie wounded and some dying. He did not know why it was, but danger made him more aware of life. It had always been like this. He'd always had to dive off the highest bridge and risk breaking his neck. He'd always been the one to tackle the most dangerous task with his buddies. Now he was in the most dangerous game of all.

"Look out—Clanton's shootin'!" Morgan Earp yelled.

A shot rang out, breaking the stillness of the afternoon.

Reb pulled his Colt .44 Peacemaker smoothly from its holster. It came out easily. In one motion he pulled the hammer back and put the sight on the figure of Billy Clanton, who was shooting as fast as he could. Reb's finger tightened on the Colt's trigger—and then the gun exploded, and he felt the revolver kick back in his hand . . .

"Wake up! Wake up, Reb. Well, how was it?"

Reb shook his head. It was an abrupt jolt coming back from the dust and gunfire and excitement of the OK Corral to find himself in the dream machine chair with Oliver sitting across from him. He shook his head. "It was great, Oliver. I just hated to quit."

"You can go back anytime you want."

"Can I do it right now?" Reb said quickly.

"I don't see why not. I don't have anything else to do. You pick your time, and I'll put you right there. You need relaxation like this, Reb. After all, a fellow needs a break from all the strain."

"Yeah, he does at that." Reb took the glass and quickly drank down the liquid. When he felt the headpiece tighten on his temples, he could hardly wait to go back into the excitement that was so lacking right now in his life in Nuworld.

Dave Cooper sat behind the wheel of the Ferrari, waiting for the starting signal. When it came, he jammed his foot on the pedal. The powerful engine roared, the wheels screamed, and he felt himself thrown back against the seat of the powerful racer as the Indianapolis 500 began. The wheel felt small in his hands. He was practically lying on his back in the low car that had been custom-made for him.

To one side, Dave saw his arch rival, Jack Starr, pulling ahead. Gritting his teeth, he downshifted to get more traction. The Ferrari hurtled forward as if shot from a gun, and he roared past Starr. But on his right a flash of light caught his eye, and then he heard the crash of a racer striking his car. Desperately he pulled away, which threw him into Starr's path. Their wheels interlocked, and he spun around. His mind whirled, and when he came out of the spin, facing the right direction, he saw Starr's car rolling over and over in flames.

Poor Jack, he thought. *He didn't make it.* He smelled the burning gasoline through the mask that he wore but could hear only the roar of the high-powered race cars that surrounded him.

Around the track he went, fighting for every inch. He saw more cars pile up, and he swung to one side. A tiny warning went off in his head, and he felt a tremor as Massengill passed him, raking the left side of the Ferrari.

As Massengill forged ahead, Dave shouted, "You can't beat me! I'll show you!" And he pushed the Ferrari to maximum speed until the whole world was a blur . . .

"Well, who won the race?"

For one moment Dave did not recognize Oliver, who sat across from him. Oliver was looking at him strangely, and he repeated the question, "Did you win the 500?"

"I . . . I don't know. You brought me back before I was ready."

"Oh, I'm sorry about that," Oliver said. "Maybe tomorrow you can go back again."

Eagerly Dave said, "Couldn't we do it now, Oliver? I was just really getting into the race, you see."

"Well, it's a little late—"

"Please, Oliver. I've got to finish that race."

A strange smile came to Oliver's lips, and he studied Dave for a moment. "I suppose it'll be all right. Here you go, then. Drink this down."

"And now we have this exclusive creation by Vidal. The model is Miss Abbey Roberts."

As Abbey stepped out from behind the curtain, the long runway stretched out in front of her. On either side, women wearing furs and diamonds sat waiting for her to make her appearance. Swinging her hips in that exaggerated walk that high-fashion models use, she came down the runway. She heard a hum of appreciation go over the audience.

Abbey reached the end of the runway, came back, stopped from time to time for different poses, and knew from the approval of the designer, standing at the curtain, that she was successful. Again and again she came out onto the runway, and each time was as thrilling as it had been the first time. *I could do this forever*, she thought.

Slowly the scene faded, and Abbey was pulled back into the present. She opened her eyes and said, "Oh, Oliver. That was so much fun! This time it was in Paris, and I was the hit of the show. They didn't even care who designed the dress. They said I was the greatest model in the world."

"I'm sure you were. Did you enjoy it that much, Abbey?"

Abbey's eyes glowed with the memory. "It's what I've always wanted to do—be a fashion model." She looked down at the dusty shoes she wore and said quietly, "I was wearing a fuschia dress and gold lamé shoes. I wish you could have seen me, Oliver."

"Well, I'm glad you like the Dream Maker, Abbey. Would you like to go back?"

"Oh, yes," Abbey breathed. "Would you mind, Oliver?"

"Not a bit. Let's put the headset on. Now, drink it down—and here we go again . . ."

The white-haired old man stared at Jake. His blunt face was seamed, and his voice quivered, but his eyes were keen with intelligence. "You did a fine job with this experiment, my boy. Where did you learn science like this?"

It was a proud moment for Jake, and he said, "Mr. Edison, I've always been interested in science. I'm so glad you let me come to work for you here at your laboratory."

"Come over here, and let me show you what I'm doing. I'm trying to make a new invention."

"What will it be, Mr. Edison?"

"Well, men have been making pictures for quite awhile, but they're *still* pictures. What I want to do," Edison said loudly—for he was quite deaf—"is to make pictures that move."

"*Moving* pictures?" Jake said. "That would be great."

"Yes, it would, but I can't seem to come up with exactly the right way to do it."

Jake said quickly, "Why don't you make a series of pictures, and then show them so fast that it *seems* like they're moving."

Edison stared at him. "Why, that's wonderful. Just the idea I needed, but you'll have to help me, Jake."

"Of course, Mr. Edison. I'll be glad to."

Jake soon found himself back in the room with Oliver, who said, "So did you help Mr. Edison invent something?"

"Sure did. Now let's go back again, and I can help Mr. Alexander Graham Bell invent the telephone."

"Anything you say, Jake. After all, you've worked hard. You need a rest and a break."

Shells were flying and bursting all around. Sarah crouched low over a soldier who was bleeding terribly from a wound in his lower arm.

"Be still," she said. "You've been badly wounded."

The soldier looked up at her with dazed eyes. "Is that you? Is it Miss Florence Nightingale?"

"No, I'm not Miss Nightingale, but I'm one of her nurses. Be still now."

The soldier looked down at his mangled arm. He said, "I'm going to die, aren't I, miss?"

"No, you're not going to die. The doctors will be here soon."

"What's your name, miss?"

"It's Sarah Collingwood."

The soldier turned his eyes away from his bleeding arm and said, "Why did you come all the way out to the Crimea? This is a dirty, nasty business. It can't be very pleasant for a young woman."

"I came out for the same reason as Florence Nightingale," Sarah said quietly. "To help do what I could for those of you who are serving your country."

The soldier gasped. "I'm glad you came, Miss Collingwood. Don't leave me."

"No, I won't do that. Now, lie quietly until the doctor comes . . ."

Oliver's voice was saying, "That was quite a dream you had—going all the way to the Crimea to nurse the English soldiers."

Sarah opened her eyes. "That war was awful. I wanted to help so much."

"You've learned a lot about Miss Florence Nightingale. She was a wonderful woman."

"Yes, she was. I'd like to be just like her," Sarah said.

"Well, Wash," Oliver greeted him, "I've been wondering when you'd come back." He opened the door wide and took the boy's arm. "Come in. I've been anxious to see you again. Tell me what you've been doing."

Wash sat down. He had forced himself to come and now wished that he hadn't. "I just hadn't much time, Oliver," he said.

"Of course. I understand you are very busy. Tell me some more about it."

After the conversation had gone on for some time, Oliver said, "Now that you're here, perhaps you'd like to take a break. All your friends have been using the Dream Maker pretty regularly."

"I—I guess so, Oliver."

"Fine. Where would you like to go?"

"I'd like to go back to New Orleans. I saw a documentary once about Louis Armstrong, how he played the horn back there in the early days."

"Yes, I've seen that. Put this on." Oliver adjusted the headset, then turned and added some colorless liquid to a glass of orange juice. "Drink this down."

"What is it?" Wash said suspiciously. "I don't like medicine."

"Oh, there's nothing to this. Just helps you relax. That way you can get into Louis's music quicker."

Wash swallowed the liquid. It had no taste and seemed to have no effect. He was as tense and finely drawn as a wire, and when Oliver sat down opposite him, Wash's back was straight and his eyes were troubled.

"Now, don't worry about this, Wash. You don't have to go."

"No, it's all right. Let's try it."

Wash was sitting on a bandstand, a trumpet player with a group of black musicians, all dressed in early twentieth-century clothes. The place was small and crowded with people, and the soloist on his right he recognized instantly as the great Louis "Satchmo" Armstrong. Wash listened, filled with admiration for this man who had been his idol back in another time.

When the solo was over, Satchmo turned to Wash

and said, "Hey, it's your turn now. Let's hear you toot that horn."

Wash looked over the audience and swallowed hard, but Satchmo said kindly, "Don't be afraid, now. Come on, let's hear you blow that thing."

Wash began to play, and soon the others joined in. He could hear Satchmo sing out, "That's the way to do it! Now, that's playing!"

Wash had never felt anything like it in his life. As others joined in, the syncopation was there, the beat was there, and he found himself carried along with the ecstasy of the music . . .

And then suddenly he was back in Oliver's room with the Dream Maker, and Oliver was watching him. "How was it?" he said. "Did you see Satchmo?"

Wash was still carried away with the moment. He had never heard anything like it. "Yes, sir, Oliver," he said. "I heard Satchmo, and he was something."

"Maybe you ought to go back and listen to him some more. A musician like you can always learn from a master."

Wash nodded slowly and said, "I guess I better do that. Yes, sir, I guess I better do it."

6

The Real Thing

"Pilot to gunner—the flak's getting pretty thick, Frank, but we've got to make it."

His goggles fitted closely over his eyes, Josh held the Dauntless dive bomber, a torpedo plane, straight on its course. He ignored the black explosive clouds and the shell bursts that flowered around them. He felt the bullets from the guns of the enemy carrier shake the plane violently.

"Right on target. Go in and get that tin can!"

Josh held to the controls tightly. The cumbersome aircraft was only thirty feet above the water, which crawled beneath him in green waves. He had taken off from the U.S. aircraft carrier *Hornet* two hours ago, and, one by one, the members of his flight made a torpedo run at the huge Japanese ship.

"Got to get it. We just got one chance." Josh gritted his teeth and poised his thumb over the release switch for the torpedo. Every gun on the carrier, it seemed, was aimed directly at him. Even as he watched, a piece of lead tore through the plastic windshield so that it spider-webbed. "Can't see where we're going, Frank," he yelled, "but I'm going to ram this tin fish right down where she lives."

The world exploded with noise, and Josh felt a bullet rake the top of his right shoulder, numbing his hand. Then he saw the target looming ahead. Desperately he pushed the control that released the torpedo.

Instantly the bomber, freed from its heavy weight, roared toward the carrier.

We're going to hit it! Josh thought wildly. He could barely see out the shattered canopy. As the bulk of the warship flashed by, he saw streaks of gunfire and could make out small figures running around the flight deck. Then, as he cleared the ship, he heard a tremendous explosion. Looking back, he saw a huge plume of smoke rise into the air, accompanied by fragments of steel.

"We got it, Frank! We got it!" he yelled. "She's gonna go down!"

He pulled the battered aircraft up as quickly as possible. The guns below still hammered, and he felt the plane vibrate as it tried to rise. But then he saw the carrier begin to list to one side. A swell of satisfaction came over him, and he whispered, "We got it. We got a whole aircraft carrier."

Then the vessel below started to fade from view. The sea turned from brilliant emerald green to a formless gray shape . . .

Josh resisted the impulse to awaken, for he longed to stay and finish his dream. But he felt the cockpit of the torpedo bomber melt away and the hard wooden chair take shape under him. He felt the headset of the Dream Maker's controls on his temples, but he remained sitting with his eyes closed.

"Come out of it, Josh."

Oliver's voice was soft but insistent. Still, Josh remained in a state of semiconsciousness. It was like those dreams that occur just before you awake, he thought. If they are pleasant dreams, you want to stay there and not come into the reality of morning.

But Oliver's hand was on his shoulder, and then Josh felt the headset being removed. Reluctantly he opened his eyes and swept the room with a glance. "Hard to come back," he muttered. "Just hit an enemy aircraft carrier with a torpedo."

"Quite a thrill, I guess, Josh." Oliver went to the window and looked out. It was early afternoon, and the late sun came through the glass, illuminating half of his face. He was carefully and neatly groomed, as always, and seemed to be lost in thought.

Curious, Josh pulled his mind back from the excitement of flying a dive bomber during World War Two. He went over to stand beside Oliver. "Is something wrong?" he asked.

Quickly the older man turned, and there was a strange smile on his face. "No, quite the contrary, Josh," he said, and the excitement in his voice caught Josh's attention.

"What is it?" Josh asked. "Have you found one of our missing people? Some kind of a clue maybe?"

"Well, I'm getting closer to that, but that's not why I'm excited."

Josh had never learned to read Oliver's moods. He was an outgoing, cheerful man, with a fund of entertaining and humorous stories. Still, at times he fell silent, and his eyes were hooded, concealing something that Josh could never fathom. Now he examined the inventor's face and saw that his cheeks were tense from some sort of strain.

"Is it trouble?" Josh asked quietly. "I'm sort of used to that. We haven't had anything but trouble since we got to this time and this place."

Sympathetically, Oliver nodded. He patted Josh on the shoulder. "I know it's been hard on all of you. It's hard on everybody on this planet. This war going on between the Dark Lord and Goél—I think everybody's had about all they can take."

He did not like to see Oliver discouraged, for he had found in their friendship a release from the strain that had been tearing him down. "Can you tell me about it?" he asked.

Oliver seemed to be weighing something in his mind. His eyes narrowed slightly as he scrutinized Josh. "I'm not sure whether I ought to tell you or not."

"Does it have anything to do with—with Goél and the battle with the Dark Lord?"

"It has something to do with *everything*," Oliver said. He smiled mysteriously, then laughed aloud. "I know that sounds odd, but it's really true, Josh." He hesitated for only one fraction of a moment, then he threw both hands out, palms upward. "Josh! You remember I told you that I was working on something big—something *really* big?"

Josh straightened up. Oliver's excitement caused him to feel some excitement too. "You mean you found how to do it?"

"I think I've got a piece of it," Oliver said slowly, almost in awe. "Josh, this is so big—it's bigger than I even dreamed it would be!"

Josh smiled. "You warned me once not to believe anything inventors said. Does that still go?"

"I *may* be overestimating what I found." Oliver began to walk around the room rapidly, slapping his hands together, bobbing his head, and muttering to himself. It was as if he had forgotten that Josh was there.

The young man stood watching, afraid to interrupt.

At last Oliver turned and came toward him, a determined set to his features. "It's something really big, though, Josh. The biggest thing I ever dreamed of, and it's going to happen. I just know it is! I can feel it in my bones." He took a deep breath. "I'm going to try to tell you about it, but I warn you—you've got to think big."

"Let her rip, Oliver," Josh said. "What is it?"

"Did you ever read any science fiction, Josh?"

"No, not very much. Just a little when I was twelve or thirteen, and most of it was over my head."

"Well, science fiction isn't really about science," Oliver said. "There's all kinds of talk about 'science,' but it isn't. For instance, in one of Edgar Allan Poe's stories he wrote about a man who traveled in a rocketship. When someone asked him how it worked, he just said, 'You wouldn't understand it.'" Oliver laughed. "They went to the moon, and the reader just accepted that there was a ship at that time that could do that. Well, you're just going to have to accept what I'm going to tell you, without a scientific explanation. It's something I've worked on all my life, and now I found it. In a way, it's all tied up with the work I've done with the Dream Maker."

"What does your new invention do?"

"Those fellows who write science fiction talk about what's called a parallel universe."

"I've heard of that. I read a story about it once. No, let's see. I saw it on a television program. It was about this man who discovered that there was another universe almost exactly like the one we're in."

"That's it!" Oliver said excitedly. "There're a lot of books about that for sci-fi readers, and I've found out that, in a way, it's true."

"But how could you find out about that?" Josh demanded.

"You see, you want scientific explanations. I can't give you any. Come, sit down, Josh, and listen. I think it's more a matter of philosophy than anything else. In any case, through the Dream Maker I've done a lot of roaming through old books. And somehow, some time ago, I broke through into what I knew wasn't anything on this planet. Most everything was the same, but some things were different. For example, I went back in time to 1994. At that time, Bill Clinton was president of the United States; but in *that* universe—the one I'd stumbled into—he lost the election to George Bush."

"But Clinton *was* elected."

"In *this* universe, yes. But not in universe number two." Oliver smiled, "It's out there, Josh, with just a few changes."

Josh sat and listened with growing excitement while Oliver talked. But he could not understand all of what was being said.

Finally Oliver cocked his head. "You don't really understand the significance of this, do you?"

"I guess I don't. What if it *is* out there? What would that have to do with us?"

"Why, don't you see?" Oliver asked, his eyes almost glaring with excitement. "Josh, we can *go* there. You could go home again. Back to the way things were."

The words seemed to hang in the air, echoing hollowly. Josh stared at Oliver. Over the man's shoulder, a beam of golden sunlight illuminated his silvery hair. Tiny dust motes swam by the millions in that beam, and suddenly Josh thought, *Why, every one of those motes could be a separate world, just like ours. I read a story about that too.* Aloud he said, "You mean we can use the Dream Maker and go into that parallel world like you did?"

"You're not thinking right, Josh." Oliver's face grew terribly serious. "What's your life been like since you came to Nuworld? You've told me about it. Danger and doubt, losing friends to death, dangerous missions. It's been nothing but hard times."

"Not all of it's been hard," Josh said defensively. "I've met some good people. I met you for one, Oliver, and a few others."

"I'm glad to hear you feel that way, Josh." Oliver smiled. "I feel that way about you too. But just think about your life in Oldworld. You had parents there. You've told me about them."

"They're both dead now," Josh said shortly. The pain from the loss of his parents still hurt him, and he did not want to talk about it.

Oliver, however, said, "But they're not dead in *that* world. You can go back and be a boy again. Your parents will be there. Your grandparents will be there. Remember the fun you used to have with them on the farm every summer?"

Memories came floating back to Josh, and he nodded slowly. "Yes, I remember."

"And you had a dog, didn't you? What was his name?"

"His name was Jock. He was the best dog a kid ever had."

"Well, Jock will be there. It'll be just like it was, Josh. How would you like that?"

Suddenly Josh thought he would give anything to go back to what life was like when he was twelve or thirteen. He had had problems then, too, but nothing like the terrible things that he'd encountered in Nuworld. Slowly he nodded again. "It would be all right. It would be great. You mean I use the Dream Maker and dream about all that?"

"No, it just doesn't seem to work like that," Oliver said. "Somehow there's a difference. You can go into books and come right back out again, or into movies, or TV, but there's something different about going into this parallel universe. Once you get there, it's not as easy to get back. I had a horrible time, and I've been afraid to go back ever since. I think, Josh, that at least *usually* the choice is either to go back and stay or you stay here."

Josh could not think clearly. "But I couldn't go away and leave my friends. And leave Goél. He's depending on us to fight. There's a big battle coming up."

"I know there is. But in that other world, that wouldn't matter. *Nuworld* would be a dream world. You would be living in reality, Josh, don't you see? All this *here* would be just a dream, a bad dream."

Something tugged at Josh. He was torn two ways. He longed to be back in those golden years in Oldworld—but he was still disturbed at the thought of leaving his friends. "I'd hate to leave my friends."

"You mean Jake and Sarah. Especially Sarah, I'll bet."

"Well, yes, Sarah. I'd hate to leave her. And the others too."

"Josh, you're still not thinking right," Oliver insisted. "*They'll* go back too. Sarah will be going back, and Jake and Reb. They'll all go back again. If you want to find them in Oldworld, you can go find Reb in Arkansas. You won't lose your friends. I'll bet you'll be better friends than ever."

"What about Goél? Will he be there?"

"It's hard to say about Goél. He's not like you or me, but if he wants to be there, he will."

"Say, that's right, isn't it?" The idea began to grow on Josh, and he got up and paced the floor excitedly. "I just don't know. It's a big decision. Are you sure we can't come back here? *You* did."

"With great difficulty. I don't think it's like trying on a suit. If you don't like a suit, you can put it back. Somehow, when you shift to that other universe, that's it, Josh. Look," he said, "why don't you go talk to your friends? See what they say."

"I'll do that. I could always talk with Sarah. She's got a level head."

"You do that. Come back and tell me. Maybe bring her here. We can all talk it over together, if you like." Oliver smiled. "I'd sure like to see that dog of yours myself."

Josh thought of the sable-and-gold collie that he had loved as much as he had loved anything in Oldworld beside people, and he whispered, "I'd sure like to see Jock again."

"Let me explain Oliver's new invention . . ."

Josh was meeting with Wash and Sarah. The other Sleepers were all scattered. "We can get to them later," Josh had said.

Sarah and Wash stood listening as he talked about Oliver's latest discovery.

"I tell you, Oliver says it can be done," Josh protested.

Sarah could see that Josh was more excited than she had ever seen him before. His eyes were bright, and he was animated and filled with enthusiasm.

"Don't you see?" he said. "We can leave all this trouble, and who knows whether we'll live another day in this place or not? We could go *home* again."

Wash bit his lip thoughtfully. "But what about Goél? What about the battle that's coming up?"

"Oh, I forgot to tell you," Josh said hastily. "You see, when we get back to that other universe, *that'll* be the reality. All this here will just be a dream."

Sarah was doubtful. "I don't see how that could be. This *isn't* a dream we're in now." She reached out and pinched Josh, who cringed and said, "Ouch!"

"See—you don't *feel* things in a dream, Josh. This is reality *here.*"

"It's too complicated to explain. I don't understand it all myself, but just think about going home again," he said. "Wouldn't that be great?"

"Well," Wash scratched his head thoughtfully, "I wouldn't mind gettin' back and having some good Oldworld cooking again. And there are folks I'd like to see back there. I miss my brother a lot, but it just doesn't sound like it could be so."

The more Josh argued, the more Wash seemed to grow adamant against the idea. Finally, Josh snapped, "Look, Wash! In this battle that's coming up, we don't know how it's going to turn out. The Dark Lord has about a hundred million troops, more or less, and we know how many there are of us. Not enough to fill a football stadium. I don't see how we can win."

Sarah said timidly, "But we've got Goél . . ."

She knew that was a stumper for Josh, for he loved and trusted Goél. He had no answer, but she saw that the pull of his homeland was so strong that he'd closed his mind to all his feelings for the one who meant so much.

"He can get somebody else," Josh said. "I want to go home. You think about it. We'll tell all the others. Wash, you go explain it to Reb. And you can tell Abbey, Sarah. I'll tell Jake and Dave, and I think we ought to all go back together. Then we'll all be in the same universe, and we can get together and have reunions. We can remember this as sort of a dream. We'll meet when everybody knows what's going on, and make our decision."

Wash watched as he left the room, then turned to Sarah. "What do you think?"

Sarah was confused. "It sounds wonderful," she

admitted, "and Josh is sure carried away with the idea."

"I'm not sure that's the real Josh," Wash said. "He's been so tired and worn out and strained that he's not thinking straight. Another thing," he said quickly, "I'm not sure all this Dream Maker stuff has been good for him."

"Well, what's wrong with it? You never have liked it, I know."

"It's like I said from the beginning. You can get hooked on things like that. It's easy. You just sit there, and Oliver puts that clamp on your head, and suddenly everything is nice and you're playing, you're enjoying, you're dreaming. It's like dope was back in Oldworld. Guys that were on drugs—they could dope out for a while and everything seemed fine." Wash frowned. "But they had to come back sooner or later. And they got to where finally it was so easy to stay doped up, and so hard to live in the real world, that they just forgot about the real world and became dope addicts."

Sarah was listening carefully. She knew that this small young man had deep wisdom that was not obvious to those who did not know him well. "I think that's right, but do you really think this is that kind of thing? I mean it's just a game."

"You remember back, just before the big war, when computers had gotten big? I had a friend that got on the Internet. It was just a game, but he kept spending longer and longer times at it. Finally, he was staying at that dumb thing for five, six, seven hours a day. School, family, nothing meant anything to him—just Internet. He was hooked on that thing like some get hooked on dope."

"And you think the Dream Maker's doing that to us?" Sarah asked.

"It could do it to me. And I can't say about everybody else, but I think it's changed Josh. He's gotten used to the easy way of dreaming. And what Oliver is saying, I think, is that we can go back to one big dream."

"But he says that's the reality and *this* is the dream."

"Well, I don't believe it," Wash said stubbornly. "And I'm not going back. I'm staying here."

Sarah sat for a long time after Wash left. She had learned to love Josh Adams, first as a young girl will admire a boy near her own age. But lately, as they were passing into adulthood, she knew that somehow it was more than that. "I want to trust Josh," she whispered, "but I'm not sure this is the right thing."

What if he goes and leaves you here?

The thought leaped into her mind, and fear along with it. "No!" she said aloud, almost in terror. "I can't let you do that, Josh. If you go back, I'll have to go back too!"

Josh talked to Jake and Dave. Both were interested but somewhat doubtful. However, Josh was so excited that they were carried away with the idea. "I'm going back to talk to Oliver one more time," Josh said. "I'll get back to you, and we'll make our decision."

"I think your decision is already made," Dave said slowly.

"Well, it sounds like a way we can keep each other, and get away from this place, and get back to what we used to have. I'll see you later."

Josh did not go at once to Oliver's house. He walked for a long time. He was really torn in two directions himself. Thoughts of Goél kept coming to him, and he remembered the kindly face and how Goél had preserved him through so many difficult times. Almost like a prayer, he said, "Goél, why don't you come now when I need you? You could tell me what to do."

But Goél did not come, and in desperation Josh knew that he would have to make his own decision.

He entered Oliver's house at the man's invitation, and for a long time the two sat talking. Josh explained his difficulty, and Oliver was sympathetic.

"I know exactly what you mean," he said. "And I can't make the decision for you."

If Oliver had tried to persuade him, Josh was ready to resist. But Oliver made no attempt to do so. Instead, he said, "You're a smart young fellow, Josh. If you don't want to go back home, that may be right for you. Some of the others may feel differently, of course."

"Wait a minute, Oliver. I didn't say I *wasn't* going back. It's so hard . . ."

"I'll tell you what," Oliver said abruptly. "I have a history book on small towns in America. Why don't you just go back to Oldworld on the Dream Maker and visit? Then we'll see. Maybe you'll get an idea about what to do."

This struck Josh as wisdom, and he said eagerly, "Yes, that's what I'll do!"

Josh found himself walking along a tree-lined street in a pleasant neighborhood. He saw his house up ahead, and his heart leaped as a large collie came out barking, his gold-and-white coat shining in the sun.

"Jock!" Josh fell to his knees, embracing the dog, who licked his face furiously, then ran around him barking sharply and pulling at his pants leg.

Then Josh looked at the house. His heart rose in his throat like a lump. He walked inside.

Immediately his mother appeared and said, smiling at him, "I've made fresh cookies, Josh, and your dad is taking you to the ball game tonight."

"That I am." Josh's father poked his head around the door and winked. "And afterwards we'll go out and get a pizza."

Josh stood still, unable to speak. His eyes suddenly filled with tears.

I'm home again, he thought and knew then that he had made his decision.

7

"I Trust You, Josh!"

The taste of his life back in Oldworld hit Josh hard. He left Oliver's and went back to his room. That night he dreamed of home again. It was not an innervision thing this time—just a simple dream of home, of friends, of fishing trips with his dad, of talking with his mother while she fixed supper. He had often dreamed of these things, but now the innervision trip had made this dream as sharp and clear as reality itself.

All the next day Josh remained close to his room. He couldn't clear his mind of thoughts of home. He had a tremendous desire to rush over to Oliver's and find his way through whatever miracle Oliver had discovered and be back on planet Earth as it was during the golden days of his childhood. He restrained himself, saying sternly, "Josh, you've got to talk to the others. You've got to convince them that going back is the right thing to do."

Still, it was difficult for him, and he waited impatiently for nightfall. As soon as dusk came, he found his way through the city to an old abandoned house outside of town. Reb had taken up residence there, camping out more or less, for the roof leaked badly when it rained.

The other Sleepers were already there, and he saw that Reb had made a fire in the fireplace. The cheerful blaze was welcome, although it was not cold outside.

Josh grinned, marching over to the fireplace and holding his hands out to the leaping yellow-and-red flames. “I always liked a fire. Wish we had some marsh-mallows and weiners. Remember those? Did all of you go on marshmallow roasts?”

“Sure did.” Wash grinned back at him. “And I always set mine on fire. Turned out to be nothing but a black cinder on the end of a coat hanger.”

Everyone laughed, and Abbey said wistfully, “Every kid in America did that. We’d always take marshmallows and weinies and buns, make hot dogs, and sit around the fire and sing.”

“I guess we all remember some of those good times,” Dave said. He was sitting on an upturned box, leaning against the wall, and his strong, tanned face caught the reflection of the fire as he turned to say, “Well, Josh, I guess we’ve got a decision to make, but some of us still aren’t too convinced about Oliver’s newfangled invention.”

Immediately Josh began to explain all the advantages of returning home to life as it was. He was usually not eloquent—indeed, he was rather shy at times. Now, however, he was overflowing with words, and he spoke with excitement. The firelight’s flicker was reflected in his blue eyes as he spoke. He ended his appeal by saying, “So, you see, we won’t really be losing anything. All of us are tired of this struggle on Nuworld. Well, we don’t have to do it anymore.”

A silence fell across the room.

It was Wash who spoke up. “I see what you’re talking about, Josh—but I just can’t buy it.”

Josh knew that Wash was the leader of the resistance against the idea of going home. Wash had never been in favor of the Dream Maker. For an instant, resentment filled Josh. *Why can’t he just go along with the rest of us?* he thought. But he was wise enough not to show his irritation. “Look, Wash, I know you’ve had some second thoughts about all this, but I don't understand them. Do you like it here with all the hard times we've been having?"

"Well, I had some hard times back in Oldworld. Some of you didn't grow up like I did. My idea of a big meal was a moon pie and a Diet Coke. I can still remember some of the places we lived in," he said slowly, his eyes thoughtful. "There was a lot of us in one little room. And we wasn't there alone, either." He shuddered. "There was rats there too. One of them bit my baby sister once." Wash looked around and saw that the others were watching him intently. That seemed to embarrass him, and he said, "I didn't mean to tell all that, but I think some of the rest of you might remember some hard times too."

"You're right about that, Wash," Jake said. "It wasn't a bed of roses for me on the lower East Side of New York. There were gangs there. They caught me one time and beat me so bad I couldn't walk for a week. I had to have six stitches taken right here." He touched his forehead where a faint scar traced over his right eyebrow. He frowned. "I wouldn't want to go back to *that* again."

Josh saw that he had to do something. "Well, sure, we all remember hard times, but you're forgetting one thing."

"What's that?" Jake asked, raising his eyebrows.

"We know each other now," Josh said. "I mean—look, Wash, I could get some money from my parents and send it to you if we're living our lives again back in that time. You could do that too, Dave—give Jake a hand. Couldn't you? We could help each other." He went on quickly explaining how they would still be the Seven Sleepers although they wouldn't have slept in the time capsules. "We can stay close to each other. We can meet, and as we grow older, why, we'll be closer than ever." He spoke again with great fervor, and finally he said, "I think we all ought to be together on this."

"Give us a day or two to think about it, Josh," Wash said.

"Why, sure. I think that's only right. It's a big decision." Josh was disappointed for he wished to make the decision now, but he saw that they were not ready. "We'll meet here again—day after tomorrow, say. That'll give us forty-eight hours. By that time we can all have thought it over."

The others agreed, and Josh thought Wash looked much relieved.

When they left Reb's place, Josh and Sarah walked along the streets together, since the room that she had was close to the one that Josh rented at the inn. The stars were shining, and Josh looked up once, saying, "I wish I knew all their names."

"You suppose there'd be different stars in that parallel universe?" Sarah asked. "I wouldn't like it if there weren't a Big Dipper." She pointed at it. "That's the only constellation I really know."

"Well, I don't know many myself, but there'll be stars there. Maybe the Dipper would be turned the other way, or maybe it will be a big dinner platter." The two laughed together at that, and Josh took her hand. "Sarah, I feel so *good* about all this! You know, you'd be back at our house like you were, and we could go skating again down at the rink. You remember that?"

"How could I not remember that? You kept falling and pulling me down with you."

"Well, I needed something to cushion my fall." Josh grinned. "You were always pretty skinny for that, but a fellow does the best he can."

"You're awful, Josh." Sarah pouted.

"Well, you're not skinny anymore," Josh said. "You've fattened up pretty nicely."

"I'm not fat!" she exclaimed indignantly.

"Well, I didn't mean that exactly. I mean you're . . . well . . . you're real nice," he said lamely. "Just like a girl ought to be. But wouldn't that be great, doing all those things together again? And there wouldn't be any war this time."

The two walked on slowly. When they got to Sarah's door, there was a moment's silence. Josh said, "I feel like we've been out on a date."

"I always wanted you to ask me for a date back in Oldworld, but I was younger than you, and you weren't interested in girls anyhow."

"That's what you thought," Josh said abruptly. "I was always interested in you. I thought you were the prettiest girl I ever saw—I still do."

"Josh, that's not so. I'm not nearly as pretty as Abbey."

"You are to me," Josh said loyally. He suddenly felt flustered. "I was always embarrassed when I thought about taking a girl out, because I knew when we got to the door like this, there'd be a tense moment."

"Why would it be tense?"

"Well, wasn't a guy supposed to kiss a girl at the end of a date?"

"Maybe sometimes. But, Josh, we were just kids then."

Josh cleared his throat. "Well, we're not kids anymore. You're a fine-looking young woman. The best I know, Sarah."

"Am I, Josh?"

Sarah looked very pretty as she stood there in the moonlight. Without meaning to, he reached over and kissed her cheek. He expected her to pull away, maybe even to slap him, but she didn't. His heart beat faster than he'd thought possible. When he drew back, he could not speak for a moment. He wanted to tell her how sweet she was and how much he cared for her, but all of his words had left him.

Sarah looked up at him. She seemed small and defenseless somehow. She whispered, "I trust you, Josh. If you want to go home again, I'll go with you."

Josh's heart seemed to pound even more, and he said huskily, "Do you really trust me that much, Sarah?"

"I know you'd never do anything to hurt me."

"No, I wouldn't." Josh suddenly felt ten feet tall. "We're going home, Sarah," he said. "Now all we have to do is convince the others."

For two days the Sleepers did little but think about the decision they had to make. They sought each other out and talked, and talked, and talked—and still were in disagreement.

Wash grew steadily more opposed to the idea. He found little support, however, even from Reb, who usually backed him. "But, Reb," he said on the second day, "can't you see? We'd be leaving Goél. Have you forgotten what he's meant to us?"

"I'm not forgetting anything," Reb said stubbornly. The bleached-blond Southerner had a mulish streak. Good-humored, full of fun, always ready to help, and generous to a fault—still, when he got his head made up, it took an act of Congress to change it. And now, he seemed to have made up his mind.

"Look, I been thinking about it. If we go back, it wouldn't be like Oldworld was. We've got to be good friends here—the best I ever had." Reb gave the smaller boy a sudden grin. "I couldn't get along without you, but I wouldn't have to. We'd be in the same world."

"Arkansas is a long way from where I grew up."

"Wouldn't matter. I used to hitchhike all over. I'd come down there and visit with you," Reb said.

"Man, you'd never get out of my neighborhood alive. Why, they'd eat you like a piece of bread!"

"No, they wouldn't do that because you're my friend. You'd have to take care of me." Reb grinned again. "You'd do that, wouldn't you?"

Wash was suddenly overcome with emotion at Reb's friendship and loyalty. "We wouldn't have been friends back in the old days. We wouldn't even have liked each other. Matter of fact, I don't think you probably liked *any* black people."

"But I didn't know you then, Wash, and I've changed my mind about black people. There's good and bad in all of us, I reckon."

"You got that right," Wash said, "and that's all we have to know. You're a mighty good friend to me, Reb Jackson."

"Well, we'd still be friends, and we could do lots of stuff together. Maybe we could bum around the country. Go to the mountains in Colorado. I always wanted to see that snow. Maybe try skiing. We'd stop and work a little bit, maybe on a ranch. I'd teach you how to rope. No telling what we could do."

He talked excitedly, and by end of the afternoon he had Wash half believing him. "You think about it, Wash. We have to make our decision pretty soon."

"All right, Reb. I'll think about it."

The two parted, and Wash walked the streets of Acton for a while. Finally he found himself standing before Oliver's door. "I'm gonna give this thing one more try," he said. He walked over, knocked on the door, and found Oliver at home.

"Come in, Wash. Glad to see you."

"Oliver, tell me some more about this other world that you're talking about."

"The parallel universe? Well, come on and sit down, but I don't think I can explain it. I don't understand it myself. It's just too big for the human mind."

"Just tell me what you think," Wash said earnestly. "Everybody's going to make a decision, and I still don't really like the idea."

"You'll have to make up your own mind, Wash, but the way I see it . . ."

Wash left Oliver's house two hours later. His head was swimming, and he felt more confused than ever. "That Oliver sure is a spellbinder!" he muttered to himself as he made his way along the darkening street.

"I feel like I'm being stretched two ways at once," Wash said aloud after he had gone to bed that night. "Part of me wants to stay here and help Goél win this here final battle he keeps talking about, and the other half of me wants to go home with the rest of the bunch." The thought of being left alone in Nuworld without the other Sleepers frightened him, and he lay awake for a long time, struggling.

When Wash did go to sleep, he had a bad dream in which he was all alone on the ocean. He was floating, and deep below were monsters with sharp teeth and tentacles and beaks that could snap his leg off in a single bite. He kept crying out, "Reb—Josh—Sarah—!" Over and over again he called the names of the Sleepers.

He woke up with a start, soaking wet with sweat and trembling with fear.

"I sure would be some lonesome dude without my friends," he whispered, and the sound of his own voice made him feel more lonesome still.

8
Standing in the Gap

The Sleepers met back at the house where Reb was camped out, and Josh eagerly asked for a vote.

"It's time to make a decision, and it's pretty simple. Either we stay here, or we go back home." He hesitated for one moment, cutting his eyes over toward Wash. "Everyone in favor of going home raise your hand."

Despite all of his good intentions, Wash still felt a strong unwillingness to enter into Oliver's plan. As soon as Josh spoke, tension seemed to build up in him. He wished that he were anywhere else in the world but in this room with the dearest friends he had. He had come to the meeting fully intending to go along with the crowd, but he just could not lift his hand. It was as if an anvil had been tied to it, and though his mind said, *Go on—raise your hand—do it!* he simply could not find the strength. He knew this was in his mind, not in his body, but that seemed to make no difference. He could not join in.

"You're the only holdout, Wash," Reb said, frowning slightly. "I thought we had just about settled this."

"Yes, Wash," Sarah said. She glanced at Josh, then back at the small black boy. "I think this is one of those times when we have to follow the leader. Sometimes we have to follow blindly. We've done that often enough."

Hating himself, Wash stared down at the floor. He felt the pressure of the wills of the others tugging at him to come along with them. Lifting his eyes, he looked at Sarah. "Yes, but that was when we were asked to follow *Goél* blindly. I don't think he could make a mistake."

"So you think I'm wrong?" Josh asked sharply.

"I think you could be this time, Josh. There's just something *wrong* with this! I don't know what it is, but it's there, and I just can't get it out of my head."

This was the beginning of a meeting that lasted for what seemed like hours. Wash sat in the middle of the group, and each Sleeper took turns trying to persuade him. The hardest to ignore was Sarah, whom he had always admired for her gentleness and wisdom. She did not yell at him—no one did, of course—still, he wished with all his heart that he could give up and say yes.

Finally, in disgust, Jake threw up his hands. "Well, that settles it. We'll just have to leave you here."

Fear came into Wash's heart, but he could not find a word to say. His throat seemed to be closing up. He got up numbly and stood looking around. These faces were dear to him, and he studied them all. Josh Adams and Sarah Collingwood. Then there was Bob Lee Jackson—his closest friend—and Dave Cooper and pretty little Abbey Roberts, whose blue eyes seemed yearning to draw him into the circle. Last, of course, there was Jake Garfield, glaring at him pugnaciously as if he wished to come over and pummel him with his fists.

"I guess you folks will want to be alone," Wash said quietly. He turned and left the room, and once he stepped outside into the darkness he had never felt so alone in all his life.

Wash slept very little that night. He was afraid to go to sleep because of the nightmares that might follow. He fought sleep by walking around and taking sips of the tepid water that was in the jug on the bedside table. Again and again he argued with himself, sometimes aloud. "You are *stupid*, Gregory Randolph Washington Jones!" he addressed himself sternly. "You think you got more sense than the other six Sleepers? You're the youngest one. They're all smarter than you are—and older. Why do you have to be such a nerd?"

The temptation became stronger than ever to run out of the room, to find Josh, and to cry, "I'll go with you, Josh. It may be wrong, but I'm trusting you."

He made up his mind that eventually he would have to do this. "I can't stay here alone," he mumbled as he lay down on his bed. His eyes were gritty, and his speech became slurred. "Gotta go find Josh . . . tell him I'll go with him and the rest . . . can't stay here alone . . ."

Warm darkness closed around him, and he dropped into a sound sleep. His mind was at rest, as was his body, and he slept dreamlessly.

"Wash . . ."

Wash stirred. His body moved, as somewhere inside his head a voice seemed to be speaking.

"Wash, listen to me . . ."

Wash knew that he was asleep, but the figure of Goél seemed to materialize before him. He could not see clearly except that Goél was standing across the room, almost hidden by the darkness. A single light came from somewhere and illuminated his strong features.

"Goél, is it you?"

"Yes, my son. Can you hear me?"

"I'm dreaming this, aren't I?"

"There's a very fine line, Wash, between dreams and reality. In any case, I'm here to give you comfort."

At once Wash knew a start of fear. "Please, Goél—you're not going to ask me to do something real hard, are you? I don't think I could take it."

Sorrow crossed Goél's face, a sorrow so deep and profound that it could not be expressed in words. His eyes were hooded, but Wash could see the pain and the grief reflected there. "All of us must face things that are difficult."

"Have you ever done that, Goél?"

There was a long silence, and the voice came in a whisper, "Yes, I've known the grief and sorrow of all mankind."

Wash, even knowing it was a dream, could not respond to this. The sorrow and pain that he saw in Goél's eyes were too great, and finally he whispered, "What do you want me to do?"

"You love your friends, do you not, Wash?"

"You know I do, Goél. Next to you, better than anybody."

"They're in terrible trouble."

"What's happened to them? Where are they?"

"They are in a prison that has bars much stronger than any steel you have ever seen. Of all the prisons that can be known, I think they are in the most secure."

"Well, we can break them out. We can get some dynamite—"

"Dynamite will not touch the heart or the mind. It can destroy bodies and things but nothing more. The prison they are in is of their own making. They must be delivered, or they will perish."

In Wash's dream, the faces of his friends floated into sight, and he saw that the faces were all filled with hurt and grief. This was not the way he had left them, and he knew then, somehow, that they had surrendered to some awful force that now had them trapped.

"Where are they, Goél?"

"They are trapped by their own hearts. They longed so for relief from the difficult things I have asked of them that they took an easy way. And the easy way is almost always the road that leads to the destruction of heart and of mind."

"It has something to do with that dream machine thing."

Goél smiled. "You are quick to understand, my son." He paused, then said, "You are the only one that can help the Sleepers, your friends. You must find them and set them free."

"Tell me how. Just tell me how to do it, Goél."

Goél was again silent for a moment. "You know by now that I do not always give total knowledge in advance to those who serve me. You must walk by faith. I will guide you, but you yourself must find the way. I will lead you, and you will know I'm there, but you must sometimes take steps out into what seems to be total darkness. And I must warn you, you yourself are in danger of the same prison that the others are in. Be careful, Wash. Be very careful. Trust only in what I tell you."

He hesitated for one moment more, and the silence seemed to fill Wash's mind and heart. "Enter into the prison where your friends lie. Only by entering into their prison can you bring them out to freedom and health and life."

"Goél, wait! Don't go!" Wash woke up to find himself crying out loud for Goél to return. He sat up in the bed and stared around in the murky darkness.

"It was all a dream. Just a dream," he said. But somehow he knew it was more than that. Goél had appeared to other Sleepers. Wash himself had once talked to Goél in a dream. He remembered it clearly. Now, as the small boy sat there wondering about the meaning of this dream, he knew fear. Yet somehow, even with the fear, came the knowledge that he was not quite alone in the room. Though he could not see anyone or hear a voice, still he knew that he had a friend.

"I'll do it, Goél," he said aloud. "I don't know where I'm going or how I'm going to get there, but I'll do it or die in the attempt!"

9
Wash Jones—Detective

Though Wash had discovered what to do through his dream of Goél, there still remained the problem of *how* to do it. He had never felt so alone in all of his life. Over the past two years, Wash had been constantly supported by his six friends—the other Sleepers—except for very short periods of time. All he had to do was reach out and touch one or lift his voice and call. Now, however, there was no one to touch and no one to call.

For one whole day he paced the floor of his small room, racking his brain for a solution. After dark he put on his coat, pulled a hat down over his eyes, and slipped out into the darkened streets of the town.

Faint stars twinkled overhead. He eyed them for a time and noted that the moon was rising. It was a mere sliver of a moon, a Cheshire-cat grin, yellow as old cheese. He wished it were a full moon, for that would have been somehow more cheerful. But on the other hand, he was glad that there were the faint stars and the glow of the yellow slice above to guide him.

When he reached the edge of town, he paused and peered down the road to where it turned. Then he turned back determinedly. "No sense going down that road," he muttered aloud. "If I'm going to find anything, it'll be somewhere back in town, but I wish I had someone to talk this over with."

"Whooo!"

"What's that?" Wash almost jumped out of his boots. Looking up, he saw the shadow of a great horned owl glide silently through the sky, and he gave a sigh of relief. He saw the huge bird drift by, then plummet downward. There was the sound of a brief struggle in the weeds of the field, then silence.

Wash shivered, for the instant death of the owl's prey seemed somehow ominous. Quickly he hurried back to his room. He had a little food stashed in a box beside his bunk—the heel of a loaf of bread, somewhat stale, two teaspoonsful of butter in the bottom of a tin, and the remains of some grape jelly. Hungrily he ate it and muttered, "Sure wish I had a moon pie. That'd go down good—and maybe a Pepsi."

Wash sat on his bed and thought hard. Somehow he had to carry out Goél's orders, and his brow furrowed as he tried and rejected half a dozen different plans. Then his head snapped up, and he whistled. "There's only one cat in this town that knows something about all the Sleepers." He stood up and started for the door, then halted abruptly. "But I sure don't trust that fellow Oliver. I don't know why. He seems friendly enough and all that. But that dream-machine stuff—it don't set well with me."

For some time he paced. Finally he said, "But I've got to go to him. He's the only one who can help that I know in this whole part of Nuworld. I can't go running to any old friends—they're too far away. It'll have to be Oliver."

He slipped out the door, noting that the moon was now high in the sky and that the stars were twinkling more brightly.

There were lights in Oliver's windows. He approached the house reluctantly, wishing there was something else that he might do, but nothing came to mind. When he got to the door, however, he had reached up to knock when an impulse stopped him.

Swiftly he glanced around—*nobody this way—nobody that way.*

Seeing the street was clear, Wash leaped off the small porch, ran to the side of the house, and disappeared into the deeper shadows. He bent low, for the windows were close to the ground. Approaching one he knew to be at the back of the house, he held his breath, hoping there was no dog. He didn't remember one. Carefully he got on his hands and knees and began to crawl.

He remembered that the room where the innervision machinery was kept had two windows, both not more than two feet off the ground. Slowly, holding his breath, he reached the first. Yanking off his hat, Wash lifted his head and peered into the room. *Bingo!* he thought, scarcely breathing. *There he is!*

Oliver sat at a table, working on some meaningless maze of wires and bulbs and knobs.

I wonder what he's going to do with that—blow up the world? Wash thought bitterly.

For what felt like an hour, he crouched in the shadows, watching. He really had no plan. Once Oliver got up and left the room, and Wash thought he had gone for the night. *No, it's not that,* he thought. *He'd have turned the lights out.*

Soon the inventor was back with a sandwich in one hand and a glass of amber-colored liquid in the other. He continued working, stopping occasionally to take a bite of the sandwich or a drink from the glass.

Wash's legs began to cramp. Finally, he saw Oliver stretch, yawn, and look around the room. Then the man rose suddenly and moved straight toward the window.

He's seen me! Wash thought. *It's time to run.* Instead, he flattened himself against the wall. To his horror, the window swung open, and Oliver leaned out. He was, however, not looking to the side but staring out at the orchard in the backyard. Wash did not move. He held his breath for what seemed like an eternity.

At last Oliver sighed deeply, then yawned again, and pulled himself back in.

Wash heard the window shut, and he drew a hand across his forehead. He was sweating despite the brisk night air, and he found that his hand was not steady.

That was a close one!

He waited, and suddenly the light went out. The room was plunged into blackness. Quickly Wash returned to the window and peered in but could see nothing. He knew Oliver's bedroom was upstairs, and a sudden notion frightened him. *I could go in*, he thought. *But if he caught me, that would be the whole ball game.*

For some time he stood, torn between the desire to go in and search the laboratory and fear that he might be caught. Looking up, he saw the light go on in the upstairs bedroom. It stayed on for perhaps fifteen minutes, then went out.

I'll give him time to go to sleep, Wash thought. *Then I'm going to burgle this place. I never been a burglar, but I guess this is a good time to begin.*

After thirty minutes passed like thirty days, Wash took a deep breath. *If I'm going to do it, I better do it quick.* He reached into his pocket and felt for the stub of a candle and the matches that he always carried.

Reaching up slowly, Wash tried the window. He half expected it to be locked, but to his great delight it swung freely open. He had it halfway when it suddenly gave a creak, sounding like a gun going off to Wash's sensitive ears. He froze where he stood. But nothing happened, and slowly he moved the window again—so slowly that it would not make another sound. When it was fully open, he stepped over the low threshold.

Squatting down, he pulled out the candle and lit it. The flame cast a ghostly gleam over the room. He was familiar with the laboratory and thought, *I don't know anything about those machines, but he keeps his books in a bookcase over beside that wall.*

He crossed the room as if he were going through a minefield. *All I need is to knock over a dish or something, and I'm dead meat.*

He did not, however, disturb anything and safely reached the bookcase. He held up the candle and read the labels on the spines of the leather-bound volumes. "*Inner Stellar Galactic Relationships,*" he whispered. "That don't mean nothing to me." He moved down the line, whispering the titles, some of them so complicated that he could not even pronounce them. In despair he shook his head. "It would take a college professor to understand this stuff."

Wash had almost given up when he came upon a book with two words printed on the spine—*Dream Machine.* "That's it," he whispered and pulled it out.

Now fearful that someone might see his light from the street, Wash moved over to a corner of the lab. Sitting on the floor with his back wedged against the wall, he opened the book and began to read. He was afraid he would find long columns of confusing figures, but instead the book appeared to be a diary. It began simply: "I have found the way to join minds with books or other forms of media. I can now put people into these artificial forms, and they will feel that they are reality."

This is it! Now all I got to do is find out if he's had anything to do with Josh and the others that are missing. He's got to, though. He's the only one that can run this thing.

Convinced that the answer lay in the book but fearful to steal it for fear of being found out, Wash read as fast as he could. It was hard going, but he was afraid to skip anything. He could hear the clock ticking in the hallway, and once there was a thump overhead that made his heart leap. He froze and waited, absolutely still, until he was convinced that there was no danger.

He had gotten only a fourth of the way through the book when he realized that there was no way that he could possibly read all of this material before dawn. In despair he thought, *Well, lots of times when I was reading a book back in Oldworld, I'd just skip to the end of it to see how it came out. I'm gonna try that now.*

Wash turned quickly to the back quarter of the book and was delighted when the first words his eyes fell on were: "The Sleepers are becoming more and more addicted to innervision. Josh, the leader, is the most likely to succumb first. He is exhausted and cannot think straight. I will have him soon. On the other hand, the small black boy is very resistant. I may have to take other steps with him."

Other steps. Other steps, my foot! I'd like to take my step and kick you back between the pockets. He read on eagerly and found records of how each of the Sleepers had come in and which book or television program they had asked to be transported into. It was fascinating, but he had no time to waste.

One scientific fact did catch his eye, though. He found a scribbled note that said, "I have found a way to put two dreamers into the same dream by installing a twin set of controls. I can put one subject into a dream and then, by attaching an identical headset, at identical settings, put another dreamer into that same dream. Thus if I put Josh Adams into a dream, I can also put the girl Sarah into that same dream. I do not know what value this is, but it has been an interesting experiment."

Instantly Wash knew what he had to do. "That's it," he whispered. "I've got to find where Josh is, and I got to get to him in his dream, whatever it is, and I got to convince him to come back."

He read a little farther, and what he read confirmed his belief. Oliver had written about something he called "final dreams": "I have so calibrated the innervision machinery that once a dreamer is put into these final dreams, he can come back only if he himself wills it. This will prevent anyone from going after others to bring them back against their will. It would be useless, for they themselves must make the decision, and of course they will not do so because they are living the dream of a lifetime. They will not choose to come back, even should someone try to convince them to do so."

Wash sat absolutely still. This seemed to be the end of his findings. *What good would it do to go into their dreams if they won't come back?* But then he seemed to hear the voice of Goél saying, "Plunge into the unknown. Dare whatever you must for the sake of your friends the Sleepers."

Wash suddenly nodded. "I'll do it!" he muttered. "I'll go into their dreams, and I'll find them. I'll find Josh first and somehow convince him that he's got to come back."

But Wash was still stumped. *I've got to find them. But where are they?* He glanced upward toward where Oliver, no doubt, lay sleeping. *He's got them hidden somewhere—I just know it. And they could be almost anywhere in this town. Not in this house, though—there's not room enough.* Another thought occurred to him. *I'll bet all those other people that have disappeared—Goél's servants—I bet they're right here in this town somewhere too, and I'll have to find them.*

Wash replaced the books, left Oliver's house, closed the window, and stationed himself across the street where he could see the inventor when he came out in the morning. He slept some until dawn, but as soon as the sun rose and touched his eyes, awakening him, he was afraid to doze off again. The air was so cool his teeth chattered. His eyes were gritty from lack of sleep. Nevertheless, he stayed awake, pinching himself when he almost slipped into a half sleep.

Finally, at 8:30, Oliver came out of the house. He was wearing his hat and coat and carrying a large briefcase. He turned right and headed purposefully down the street.

Wash followed with some difficulty. He had to keep out of sight, for if Oliver turned around and saw him, the game would be up. He was also afraid that some of the townspeople would see him sneaking through alleys and dodging in and out from behind trees. That could be deadly too, for the Sanhedrin had spies everywhere.

Fortunately, Oliver did not go far. He entered a big four-story building made of dull red brick. It had a steep-pitched roof and was the largest building in Acton. Wash knew well what it was.

It's the prison—he's got them all in the old prison.

The Sleepers had learned quickly that there was a prison in Acton where criminals of all kinds were kept—not just lawbreakers from the town itself but from all the territory round about. The prison had a bad reputation, evidently well earned. According to some reports, there were murderers and thieves and every sort of tough in the world behind those red walls.

Now, Wash thought in despair, *I got to break into jail. Bad enough trying to break out. I wish Reb was here with me.*

He lurked around until Oliver came out nearly four hours later. Wash followed the inventor to his house, made certain that he was inside, and then went walking down an alley.

"How do you get into a jail?" he said. He had absolutely no idea, but he was a sturdy young man, this Wash Jones, and determined to get inside even if he never got out again.

It took Wash two days to get into the jail. He discovered that bread was delivered every morning by a dull-witted young man who brought it from across town in a cart. Wash noticed both mornings that a guard would let him in and leave the door open until the boy came out again.

Wash thought about what he did. *He lets the boy with the bread in, takes him to someplace inside, lets him deliver the bread, then brings him right back out again,* he thought. *What I've got to do is be right near that door when that bread boy goes in. I'll wait and give 'em time to get to wherever it is they take the bread. Then I'll dart inside and hide.*

It was a desperate scheme, and Wash had little hope of it working. "But it's all I know to do," he said. "If they catch me, then that's the end of it."

The next morning he timed his walk so that he was there when the bread boy came, whistling a tuneless song. The door opened at the boy's knock, and he stepped inside carrying the huge box of bread on his shoulders. Through the half-open door Wash saw the boy disappear, being led by a guard.

Quickly Wash stepped inside and gave a sigh of relief when there was nobody else in sight. A long hall led from the foyer, and he took it at once, his heart beating fast. As he came to the bottom of stairs, he saw that the first floor was divided into two sets of cells, one on each side of the hall. He peeked into a cell and saw a prisoner lying flat on his back, dressed in a dirty gray uniform.

Yanking his head back, Wash thought, *They can't be in this place.*

He got to the second floor, then to the third, and was feeling discouraged when he came to the stairs that led to the top floor. He heard footsteps coming and in desperation scrambled up the steps. The door at the top was unlocked—he stepped inside and shut it behind him, breathing hard. He turned around, and, in the faint light given by lanterns mounted from the ceiling, he almost stopped breathing.

Along both sides of the room were single cots. On each cot a person lay, and attached to his temple was a headset. The wires led to black boxes such as Wash had seen on the dream machine.

Quickly he moved down the aisle between the two lines of cots, looking at faces. Most were strangers, but on one cot lay his friend Josh Adams. He checked the other cots in the large room and breathed a sigh of relief. *They're all here.* He stopped by Reb, whose face was composed into a dull look, seeming almost dead. Leaning over him, Wash said, "Don't you worry, Reb. I'll get you out of this."

He walked back to Josh, thinking, *I'll have to get Josh to come back first. He's the leader. He'll have to bring back the rest.* “Come on, Goél,” he said, “give me some help!”

He found that each box was indeed equipped with two headsets. He read the dials, which were meaningless, then looked at Josh’s face. Josh was half smiling, but he did not look good at all to Wash. Clipping the unused headset to his own head, he lay on the floor beside Josh’s cot. He reached up to where there were two toggle switches. The one connected to Josh’s side was flipped to the “On” position; the other, which was attached to his own headset, was on “Off.”

Wash put his finger on the switch and muttered, “Well, here I come, Josh, wherever you are . . .”

10

"You're Not Real!"

The red-and-white cork floated serenely, bobbing slightly on the waves of the small creek. The blue sky and brilliant yellow sun reflected on the surface, breaking it up into long, wavy lines of light.

Suddenly the cork disappeared with a loud *plop*.

Josh Adams had been leaning back, dreamily holding the fishing pole lightly in his hands. The warm sun and the soft breeze and the murmuring of the creek had almost put him to sleep. Now, as the pole bent in his hand, he straightened up with a yell.

"Look out!" The line jerked madly, drawn by the frantic struggles of a fish trying to escape. Josh's straw hat fell off, and as the pole bent farther he yelled, "Got you! You won't get away this time."

Josh moved down the bank, giving the fish line to keep him from breaking it. It was such a powerful fish that he was afraid it would snap the pole, but finally he drew it in. His heart almost stopped as he saw the size of the bass.

Without breathing, he reached over and stuck his thumb inside the massive mouth. The fish bit down hard, but Josh didn't care. He fell over backwards and gave the fish a heave. Instantly he was up, running to where the fish was flopping, its silver scales flashing in the sunlight. Josh picked up the fish and removed the hook. The bass fought madly, but Josh held it tight.

"Must weigh five pounds at least! The biggest I ever caught!" Josh breathed.

Any fishing after that would have been anticlimactic, so he got his box of crickets and another of worms, wound up his line, and started back toward the road. He walked through the woods easily, his long legs pumping, his straw hat tilted back on his head. He was wearing a pair of faded blue jeans and a blue-and-white checked shirt open at the throat. His worn sneakers flapped as he moved.

He came out of the woods onto the road. Turning right, he found his bicycle and carefully tied the fish across the handlebars. Balancing his pole and stringing the bait buckets, he shoved off and pumped his way along. He whistled a song everyone else had stopped whistling a year ago, but he didn't care.

Josh Adams was happy. He pulled up in front of a white frame house and pushed the bicycle to the backyard, where he leaned it against a sycamore tree. He untied the fish and admired it. "Wait until Mom sees you! This'll feed everybody tonight."

Going to the door, he called out, "Mom, look what I got."

Mrs. Adams opened the screen door and looked out. She smiled. "Why, Josh, that's the biggest fish you ever brought home."

"Start making hush puppies, Mom. Make enough for Dad and me both. He never leaves me enough."

"All right." Mrs. Adams laughed. "You dress that fish. Your dad will be home early today."

Josh quickly took the fish to where he usually cleaned his catches. Pulling a knife out of a tackle box, he quickly filleted the fish and admired the pinkish meat. "Boy, I'm sorry to spoil your day, but you're gonna go down pretty good."

By the time Josh had showered and come downstairs, he heard the front door slam.

"Hi, Josh." His father grinned and threw his arm around the boy's shoulders. "I've got a surprise for you."

"I got one for you. What's yours?"

"You first."

"Well, I caught the biggest bass I ever got. We're gonna have fish and hush puppies and fries. Mom's cooking them right now. Now, what's your surprise?"

"We're going to the ball game tonight over at Bluff City."

"That's great, Dad!"

"Let me go get cleaned up. We'll eat, and we'll go—just you and me. Your mother doesn't like baseball anyway."

Josh and his parents enjoyed the fish, and his mother refused to accept help with the dishes. "You two go on now, but be back early. You've got school tomorrow, Josh."

The home team won. Then Josh and his dad stopped on the way back at a Baskin Robbins. Josh filled up on Rocky Road ice cream. His father took vanilla, and Josh said, "Only wimps eat vanilla, Dad."

"You eat your old messed-up ice cream. The only good ice cream is vanilla," Josh's dad said solemnly.

When Josh had gone to bed, he thought, just before dropping off to sleep, *What a good day. I wish every day could be this much fun!*

The next morning Josh left for school, stuffing a biscuit into his mouth. He started walking rapidly, for he was a bit late. He was still thinking of the fish he had caught.

"We shouldn't have eaten that fish. I should have had him stuffed," he said out loud.

"Josh—"

Josh was surprised, for he had not seen anybody. He turned and saw a boy smaller and younger than himself—a black boy wearing rather strange-looking clothing. "Hi," Josh said. "Are you lost?"

"No, I'm not lost."

"Well, you don't live around here, do you?" Josh said. "I haven't seen you before."

"No, I don't live around here."

All of a sudden, something struck Josh as peculiar. "How did you know my name was Josh?"

"I know a lot about you. I know your dog's name is Jock. I know you like Western movies, especially those with John Wayne—the old ones . . ."

"How did you know all this stuff about me?"

"Josh, we've got to talk."

"I can't talk to you. I've got to go to school. Don't you?"

"This is more important than school."

"I don't even know you."

"Yes, you do. You know me, and I know you. My name is Wash Jones."

"I never knew anybody named Wash." He walked rapidly away, but he heard the sound of footsteps following. Josh looked around and saw that there was an anxious, almost agonized, expression on the boy's face.

"Look," the boy said, "this means a lot to you. More than anything in the world."

"I don't believe any of this," Josh said, but he was curious. Something about the boy troubled him, and he suddenly realized what it was. He scratched his head and asked, "Have we ever met before? You look familiar."

Wash grinned faintly. "Yes, we've met before, but not like you think. Look," he said again, "we've got to talk, Josh. Please just give me a chance to tell you about something real important."

"Well, go ahead."

The boy looked around almost frantically. They were standing in the middle of the sidewalk; this was no place to talk. "Not now," he said. "After school. Will you meet me down at the creek where you caught the bass?"

"How do you know I caught a bass?" Josh asked suspiciously. "I didn't see you there."

"Just be there," Wash said. "I'll wait for you."

Josh watched as the boy walked off. Something about their meeting disturbed him. "There's something *strange* about that guy," he said. "I won't be there today. He's some kind of a kook."

Wash paced back and forth by the creek. He was more nervous than he had thought possible. "How am I going to convince Josh that what I'm telling him is true? He thinks all this here is real. But I've got to do it." He looked up, saw Josh, and drew a sigh of relief. *Well, at least he came.* He waited until the tall boy came to stand within five feet from him and said, "Thank you for coming, Josh."

Josh Adams shook his head. "I must be losing my mind! I'm going nutty. I almost didn't come. But if I didn't, I had an idea you'd show up on my doorstep. Now, what do you want?"

Wash swallowed hard. "I know this is going to be a little bit complicated. Can we sit down here beside the creek while I tell you what I've come for?"

"I don't have all day," Josh said. Then he must have seen the pleading look in Wash's eyes. He said, "All right, I'll give you ten minutes."

"Thanks, Josh." Wash sat down and folded his

legs, facing the other boy. He had been practicing his speech all day long. It sounded feeble and not possible even to his own ears, but desperately he plunged ahead.

"One time, Josh, there was a war. A big war—so big it destroyed almost the whole earth, but there were a few who were saved out of it. There were seven young people . . ."

Josh looked skeptical as he began to listen, but the intensity of Wash's expression and the strangeness of his story apparently caught his interest until finally he seemed enthralled. He leaned forward, listening to the stories of the Seven Sleepers.

Forty-five minutes later, Wash said, "And so you see, I've come to get you to come back to Nuworld with me, Josh. You've got to come." He waved his hand around. "All this that you see isn't true. It's just a dream, Josh. Your real life is back in Nuworld."

"You're a spellbinder—I'll have to say that much for you." Josh took a deep breath, grinned, and shook his head. "I never heard such a story in all my life! Do you read a lot of sci-fi?"

"I don't read *any* sci-fi," Wash said desperately. "It's true, Josh. It really is."

Josh blinked with surprise. "You really believe all this, don't you? You're not just making it up."

"Why would I want to make it up?"

"I don't know, but I don't buy it." Josh got to his feet and laughed. "I wish I could make up stories like that. You ought to write a book. You could call it *The Seven Sleepers*. Nobody'd ever believe it, of course, but the world needs good fantasy like that. Well, thanks for the story, Wash. I'll see you. Don't come back, though. I've had about all I can take of this."

Wash got to his feet too, and as he watched Josh

stroll away he said, "Well, that tears it. That was my best shot."

Be faithful.

The words came almost audibly, and Wash knew that they had not originated with him. "Be faithful?" he said aloud. "Josh won't ever believe me, not in a million years."

Be faithful. Never mind whether you win or lose. Be faithful.

Wash turned back to the creek. He looked down into the clear water and thought for a long time. Finally he said, "All right, I'll be faithful, but I don't think it's going to work."

Josh came awake with a start. Some sound had jarred on his nerves, and when he sat up in bed he was suddenly wide awake, for he saw by the moonlight that his window was opening slowly.

A burglar! he thought. For a moment he could not move, then he slipped out of bed and looked for a weapon. The window was now wide open, and a shadowy form suddenly blotted out the moonlight and stepped into the room. In desperation Josh threw himself at the form. There was a rattling crash as he drove the intruder into a lamp. It shattered, and Josh began to yell, "Help—Dad, help!"

The intruder was struggling violently, but Josh held on. Fortunately, Josh was much stronger. He was surprised at the size of the burglar, for he had no trouble at all holding him.

Suddenly the lights came on, almost blinding Josh.

"What's going on here?"

"A burglar, Dad," he cried. "Look, I caught him—he came in through the window."

Mr. Adams stepped inside the room. "A burglar,"

he said, looking down at the two. He stared at the intruder, who looked back at him, and he said, "He looks mighty young to be a burglar."

Josh's stare focused on the burglar that he had captured. "It's you," he said. "What're you doing here?"

"Josh, do you know this boy?" Mr. Adams demanded.

"Well, not exactly," Josh said. He held onto Wash's arm tightly. "Don't you try to get away now."

"I won't try to get away," Wash said quietly. "I just came to talk to you again."

"How do you know this boy? Does he go to your school?"

"No, he doesn't go to my school," Josh said. He looked over his father's shoulder and saw his mother come in. "Mom, go call the police. We've got a burglar."

Mrs. Adams looked down at the black boy. "What's your name?" she asked quietly.

"Wash Jones."

"Did you really come into this house to steal?" Mrs. Adams asked.

"No, ma'am, I didn't."

"Of course, he did," Josh said. "Look, he met me when I was going to school this morning. Said he had to talk to me. Well, I wouldn't talk to him then, but he begged me to meet him after school. So I did, and he told me some awful tale. Didn't make any sense at all, but I know what he wanted. He'd been casing the house so he could get in and burgle the place."

Mr. Adams studied the face of the intruder and sighed. "Well, I'm afraid we'll have to call the police. You did break and enter."

"But, dear—" Mrs. Adams began.

"We won't press charges, but the police need to know about things like this. He doesn't look like a burglar," Mr. Adams said, "but it's what we'll have to do."

Josh expected the boy to protest, to beg, or to threaten, but he didn't. He just turned and looked at Josh quietly. Something about his big brown eyes troubled Josh, and he could not meet his gaze. "You shouldn't have tried to come in the house. What'd you do it for?" When he got no answer, this troubled him even more. He looked at his dad and said, "Maybe we ought to just let him go. Tell him to stay away."

But Mr. Adams said, "No, he may have committed other burglaries. We don't know. Where are your parents?"

"I don't have any."

"Oh, dear!" Mrs. Adams said.

But there was no changing her husband's mind. Mr. Adams called the police, and very shortly two uniformed patrolmen appeared at the front door.

Josh stood watching, biting his lip, as Mr. Adams explained the situation.

One of the policemen said, "We'll take care of it, Mr. Adams. Come along, you."

The policeman looked very big, and Wash Jones looked very small as they disappeared. Josh stood at the door, and when they were in the car, Wash suddenly turned and looked back at him. He still had not said a word or asked for anything, but something in that look caught at Josh.

"He sure didn't look like a burglar, but you can never tell. Appearances can be deceiving. Are you sure you didn't know him, Josh? Before today, I mean?"

Josh started to answer his father, but something kept him from it. He wanted to say no, yet somehow that did not seem quite true. He tried in vain to think where he might have seen the boy, but he could not remember. "What will they do to him, Dad?"

"Well, he's a juvenile. He'll go to a reform school if they find him guilty of anything, I suppose."

This distressed Josh no end, but he knew that there was nothing he could do. He returned to his room and went to bed, but there was no sleep for him the rest of the night.

Somehow Josh had ceased to find happiness in the things he usually enjoyed. Jock tried to get him to play, but he would shove the dog away, saying, "Get away, Jock, don't bother me." He had gone back twice, trying to fish, but there was no fun in that either. All he could think of was the face of Wash Jones.

His parents noticed that Josh was moody and talking very little.

"Are you unhappy, Josh?" his mother asked quietly one day. "You don't seem yourself."

"No, I'm all right, Mom."

He was not all right, however, and for four nights he lay awake as long as he could, racking his brain. "I knew him *somewhere*," he would say. Then he would go off to sleep, and in that sleep would come the dreams. He would dream that he and some other young people were under the ocean, riding on strange shark-like creatures—or they would be fighting with dinosaurs.

"These are those crazy stories that kid told me," he said. "That's why I'm dreaming about them. But they're so *real!*"

He grew angry at himself. "I've got to forget about him," he said. "He's either a crook or he's crazy, and I don't want to have anything to do with him."

One day his father found him sitting in the backyard, staring off into space. They talked about different things for a long time, and finally he said, "Josh, you're not yourself."

"I'm all right, Dad."

"No, you're not. I don't know what's troubling you. Do you think you can tell me?"

"I—I guess I'm worried about that guy that broke into the house. I'm not sure he was a burglar."

"I'm not either. At the hearing he made no defense at all."

"The hearing? You went to the hearing, Dad?"

"Yes, I did. I even put in a good word for him, but he had a pretty strict judge. He'll be sent to a reform school upstate, I think."

"I wish I hadn't caught him."

"Josh, I can't tell you how to feel. You did what most people would have done. Now maybe it's time for you to be a friend to this boy."

"What can I do?"

"Maybe go visit him. Write him a letter, perhaps. Tell him you're his friend." Mr. Adams laid a hand on Josh's shoulder. "You've always been straight with your friends, Josh. Be straight with this Wash too."

Wash was sitting in his cell with four other boys about his own age. Three of them had just come in. They were cursing and talking loudly about a burglary they had pulled. Wash tried to pay no attention to them.

He looked up when he heard his name called. "Jones, you got a visitor."

Wash could not believe his ears. "A visitor? Me? Are you sure?"

"Come on," the guard said. He was a big, burly man and had an irritated look on his face. "If you're coming, come along."

Wash followed the guard down the hall. The keeper opened the door and said, "In there. You've got thirty minutes."

When Wash stepped in, he saw Josh Adams standing there. Josh's face was pale, and his fists were clenched. He was staring at Wash in a strange way.

Wash swallowed and said, "I'm glad to see you, Josh."

Josh Adams stood so still and for so long that Wash was afraid that he had come to berate him again. The boy did not look natural.

"Wash, are you telling me the truth?"

"Yes, it's all the truth, Josh."

The statement seemed to tear Josh in two. "What do I do then? What *can* I do?"

"You can go back to Nuworld," Wash said simply. He repeated the instructions that he had read on how to break off a dream, and he said, "But you have to do it yourself, Josh. I can't do it for you."

Josh Adams stood silent for a long time.

Wash waited quietly, knowing that the future hung in the balance for him and for the work of Goél—maybe for Nuworld itself. If Josh didn't go back, none of the other Sleepers would be freed. Maybe the Dark Lord would win after all.

Josh suddenly put out his hand. "All right," he said hoarsely, "let's go home."

Wash took the boy's hand and held it tightly with both of his. "I know it's hard, Josh," he whispered, "but you'll know soon. This place isn't real. You're going to where you're supposed to be. Now, here's what we do . . ."

11

A Calico Dress

Josh looked around at the Sleepers, their faces pale, lying on the cots, then turned to face Wash. "Well," he said quietly, "it's all true."

"You didn't have to come back, Josh," Wash said. "I know that it would have been real easy to stay there. But remember, that place wasn't real. It was just a pleasant dream."

Josh stared at the small boy, who had explained how he, alone, had resisted Oliver and his Dream Maker, and how he had, through his own efforts, found the way to bring Josh back. "You're something, Wash," he said, his voice tinged with admiration. "You're the toughest one of the Sleepers."

Wash had to feel a surge of pride at the praise. Josh knew he had felt at times that he didn't amount to much, for he was the smallest and the youngest.

Now he grinned. "I'm glad I could do it, Josh." He too glanced around, then said, "But we've got to get the rest of 'em back quick. I don't know how often they check on this place, but if Oliver comes back and catches me here, and you up walking around, he'll know something's wrong."

"I know it. Now, tell me again how it all works." He listened carefully as Wash explained, then he made an instant decision. "I want you to go get Reb back. You're his best friend. You two are closer to each other than any of the rest of us are."

"Sure, I was hoping I'd get to go after Reb. What are you going to do?"

"I'm going to go get Sarah. I got her into this," he said soberly.

"Do you have any idea at all what sort of dream she had?"

Josh had thought about this at some length. "I doubt that the dream machine let her go home. She always liked to read books and watch TV programs about farm life. She was always looking for novels about things like that." He straightened his shoulders and said firmly, "Well, now it's up to me to try and get her out—wherever she is. And like you say, we've got to get this done quick. You just attach this headpiece and throw the switch?"

"Better lie down first, or I think you'd probably fall over and maybe bust your head," Wash said. "Good luck, Josh." He put out his hand.

But Josh ignored the hand and gave him a quick hug.

"Good luck to you. Reb's a stubborn outfit. It'll take all you can do to get him to come back. If I know Reb, he's in the midst of some wild, dangerous adventure."

"What do you think Sarah's doing?"

"I have no idea. Sarah was always so quiet, but wherever she is, whatever she's doing, I'll do my best."

Josh stepped over beside the sleeping Sarah and looked down at her still face. Without another word he picked up the headset, lay down beside her cot, reached up, and pulled the switch.

Josh awoke to the sound of water running and thought at first it might be the stream where he caught the bass. But when he sat up, he knew that this was a place he had never been. There were blue-tinged mountains over to the north and another long ridge to the south. He was in a valley, and a road led toward the mountains on his right.

"This is Sarah's world all right—just the sort of place she always said she wished she'd lived in," he murmured. "Always said she'd like to live in a place without cars and TV. I'll bet she'll be around here somewhere."

He began walking down the dusty road. A bluebird flew by, a brilliant patch of color, and he watched it fly to a fence post and disappear into a hole.

He must have walked for more than an hour. The road had grown steeper until finally he was in the mountains. He grew thirsty and drank from a small stream, flat on his stomach. The water was so cold it hurt his teeth.

Getting up, he said wryly, "These dreams are sure realistic. I know I'm not here—I'm really lying flat on my back in Nuworld. Sure does *seem* real. If they could've marketed this thing as a game years ago, somebody would've gotten rich."

He had not gone more than a quarter mile farther when suddenly the road curved and he saw a house and barn sitting back from the road. A boy was working in a garden.

Somehow Josh knew that this was the dream that Sarah had chosen. She'd shown him pictures from history books of houses just like this one.

Josh walked over to the boy, who stopped hoeing beans and turned to him.

"Hello," Josh said. "Suppose I can get a drink of water?"

"Sure thing." The boy was not as tall as Josh. He wore a pair of faded blue overalls and was barefooted.

His hair was blond, and he had a pair of guileless blue eyes. "Come on up to the house. I think maybe we got some fresh buttermilk."

"Well, that would be good," Josh said. He'd always loved buttermilk, and even if this was just a dream, he determined to enjoy this imaginary treat.

As they walked toward the house, a large rambling place that could've stood some paint, Josh said, "How are the crops this year?" He had no idea about crops, having never been a farmer, but he had heard people talk about them on television.

"Well, the corn's doing good. It needs some rain, though. Are you from around these parts?"

"Oh, no. I'm from pretty far away. My name's Josh Adams."

The boy stared at him. "Adams? You any kin to Harold Adams over at Pine Ridge?"

"No, I don't think so. I'm new to these parts."

"My name is Robert Faulkner—but folks call me Rob." For one moment the young man hesitated, then asked, "Are you from Chicago—or New York?"

"Neither, Rob. Why do you ask?"

"Oh, no reason—except you talk funny." Rob looked down at the ground, kicked a stone, then lifted his blue eyes to Josh. "I'm going to the big city someday. Going to go to school and learn how to be a doctor."

"Well, that's real fine, Rob."

"Don't tell my ma. I don't want her to know it."

"Why don't you want her to know?"

"Nobody in my family ever went to school much. Ma and the rest of the family would think I was uppity if they found out." He stopped suddenly, "I don't know what I'm telling you this for. I never told anybody else."

"I won't mention it."

"Well, come on into the house. I'll see if I can get that buttermilk."

Josh stepped into the house and instantly was face to face with a tall, strong-looking woman who said, "Who's this, Rob?"

"This here's Josh Adams. He was walking down the road and asked for a drink of water," Rob replied. "I told him we might have some buttermilk. Could he have some, Ma?"

"Did you ever know of us refusing a stranger hospitality? Of course, he can have some buttermilk."

Josh smiled. "Thank you very much, Mrs. Faulkner. Always was partial to buttermilk." He took the glass that Rob brought to him and then happened to glance at a newspaper lying on the table. The headline said, "Garfield Elected President." Leaning down, he saw the date on the paper—November 1880.

When Josh straightened up, Mrs. Faulkner asked, "You from around these parts? You don't look familiar."

"No, ma'am."

"Your people from around here?"

"Well, not exactly," Josh stammered. He didn't want to lie, but of course he could not tell the whole truth either. Suddenly he had an idea. "Actually I'm looking for a girl who might have come this way. She'd be about fourteen, fifteen years old, and she's got brown eyes and real black hair."

"Ain't no strange girls like that come down our way," Rob replied. "We don't get many strangers around here. We'd sure notice a girl like that."

"What you got to do with this girl?" Mrs. Faulkner asked.

"Well, she's a real good friend of our family, and I thought she'd come to visit over in this part of the country. Wasn't sure where, and since I was close I just thought I'd stop and ask."

Something about his words seemed to trouble the woman. She stared at him and said, "So you just start out walking through the mountains asking strangers if they seen her?"

Josh felt miserable. He knew the story sounded terrible. "Well, actually it does sound kind of foolish, doesn't it? But I didn't know hardly what else to do."

"Are you aimin' to go on? It's gonna be dark before long. There ain't no towns down that way."

"I guess I'll have to," Josh said lamely.

"You better stay over the night," Mrs. Faulkner said. "My husband, he'll want to talk to you, and maybe some of the neighbors will have seen this girl. What did you say her name was?"

"Sarah. Sarah Collingwood."

"Never heard of no Collingwoods in this part of the world," Mrs. Faulkner said. "You better stay. You can take supper with us and sleep up in the attic with Rob there."

"I'll show you around when you finish that buttermilk," Rob said.

The two boys went outside, and Rob showed Josh around the farm. "We got a new calf," he said. "Aim to sell it when she gets big. Take her to the county fair." Then he repeated, "I'm hoping to go off to school some day—but don't see how that'll be."

Josh suddenly smiled. "You'll make it, Rob. You'll go to college, and you'll become a great doctor."

Rob Faulkner stared at him. "What makes you say a thing like that?"

"I just know you're going to do it."

Rob Faulkner's lower lip trembled. "That's the first

time anybody's ever told me that I can do something like that. Sure hope you're right."

The two boys spent all afternoon together. Rob Faulkner shared his dreams with Josh, and Josh enjoyed being with him.

As they went back to the house, Rob said, "Time for supper. I think we're late."

The two boys mounted the steps and went at once into the kitchen, where Mrs. Faulkner said, "You two sit. How come you stayed out so late?"

"We just got to talkin', Ma," Rob said. "He's a mighty good fellow to talk to."

"I suppose so." Mrs. Faulkner gave Josh an odd look, then turned and called, "Supper time!"

A medium-sized man with bright eyes came into the kitchen, and Rob said, "This is my pa. This here's Josh Adams, Pa."

"Glad to know you, Josh. I hear you're looking for a young gal."

"Yes, sir, I am."

"Well, we'll go ask some of the neighbors if they seen any Collingwoods."

He had no sooner spoken than the room was filled with young people—Rob's brothers and sisters, Josh supposed.

Josh, however, had eyes for only one of them. *Sarah* had come into the room. She stared at him shyly and did not say a word but took her place at the table. She was wearing a faded calico dress, and her hair was plaited in pigtails in a way he had never seen it done.

Mr. Faulkner said, "Everybody sit, and I'll ask the blessing." Then he said, "Now, let me name the children here."

Josh scarcely heard the names.

When Sarah's name was called, she lifted her eyes and looked at him.

Rob said, "Well, this ain't the Sarah you're looking for, but the one you described must look kinda like her. Black hair and brown eyes."

Josh smiled. "I'm glad to know all of you."

The meal began, and Josh was asked more questions than he could possibly answer. It took every creative power he had to keep from giving up. Since this was just a dream, he decided it wouldn't be wrong to embroider the truth some, so he made up a background for himself and tried to remember what he said.

After supper, all the children pitched in and did the dishes, then sat on the front porch and listened to the frogs bellowing down at the pond.

"That's a big bull frog," Rob said. "We could go frog giggin' if you want to."

"I wouldn't mind," Josh said. "Never have done that, though."

"Well, come on. I'll show you how."

"I want to go too," Sarah said.

Instantly the other children began begging to go.

In the end, Sarah and Rob took Josh. Frog gigging, he discovered, consisted of sitting in a boat and stabbing frogs with a long pole that had a small pitchfork-like apparatus on the end. He could not imagine eating frogs, and he said nothing as the sack grew full.

The moon was overhead when they started back.

Josh had noticed Sarah turning her dark brown eyes on him from time to time, studying him strangely. Finally she asked, "Have I ever seen you before?"

"Why? Do I look familiar?"

"Sure do. We don't see many folks around here. Real quiet in this mountain."

"You like it in the mountains, Sarah?"

Rob was up in the prow of the boat, paying little attention to the conversation. From time to time he would spear a frog and stick him into the tow sack.

Josh and Sarah talked for some time, and Josh discovered that, as he had suspected, Sarah had picked a time and a place where there were no pressures. *I knew Sarah would dream about a place like this. She can be a little girl wearing a calico dress and not have any dragons or monsters or any of the Sanhedrin coming after her. I can't say as I blame her much. I did the same thing.*

They went back to the farm and cleaned the frogs by lantern light.

Josh said, "Do you really eat these things?"

"I'll show you in the morning," Rob said. "We'll have eggs and frog legs. Ain't nothing like it, is there, Sarah?"

"They're very good." Sarah smiled at Josh. "I hope you'll find your friend."

"Oh, I think I will," Josh said, looking fondly at her.

Josh found a reason to stay on at the Faulkners. It was quite simple. He said his good-byes after breakfast the next morning, then pretended to fall down the front steps. He sat there holding his ankle.

"Well, you can't walk on that ankle," Mrs. Faulkner said firmly. "You'll have to stay until it heals up."

"I'll be happy to work to pay for my keep."

"We don't charge our guests for their keep," Mrs. Faulkner said stiffly.

Josh made the most of it. He had practiced a limp, and Rob even whittled a cane for him. He was glad this was just a dream. He wouldn't feel right about really deceiving anybody.

The next four days he spent almost entirely with Sarah and Rob. Of course, they had their farm work to do, but still Josh and Sarah had many hours together.

Sarah was Sarah, Josh discovered. She was in a dream, but there was the same sweetness and goodness in her that had always been there. He knew that somehow he had to break the news to her that she was living something that wasn't real. He began by telling her tales of the Seven Sleepers. That had worked when Wash had done the same thing with him.

On the third day he told her how Reb had slain a dragon at Camelot and had been rescued by a princess.

"Oh, that's the best story I ever heard," Sarah said. "I wish it were true. Wouldn't it be nice if things like that really happened?"

Suddenly Josh knew that the moment had come for the truth. He leaned forward and said, "Sarah, you've only known me a short time, but I'd like to think that you know a little bit about me."

"I know you're—very nice." Sarah's cheeks reddened, and she could not meet his eyes.

"I wouldn't do anything to hurt you for all the world," he said, "but I want to tell you something. Something that you're going to find hard to believe."

Startled, Sarah looked up at him, her dark eyes wide. "Why—what is it, Josh?"

"All these stories I've been telling you about the Seven Sleepers—"

"Yes?"

"They're true, Sarah."

"True? They can't be true, Josh."

"You know about the girl named Sarah that I've told you so much about in these stories?"

"Yes, you like her a lot. I can tell by the way you talk about her."

"Yes, I do like her a lot," Josh said. He reached over and took her hand and said quietly, "Sarah, I look real familiar to you, don't I? You think you know me from somewhere."

"Why, how did you know that?"

"Because, Sarah, you *did* know me, and you *do* know me. The stories are true." Josh began to speak rapidly, still holding her hand, and he saw a change come into her face as he told of some other adventures they had had together.

"I've had these dreams," she said finally. "Dreams about all these things that I couldn't understand. Why, I dreamed once that I was in a place where there were Amazon women."

"You were in that place, Sarah. You're dreaming *now. That* was the reality."

She appeared to be totally confused.

Josh said, "It'll take a while. We'll talk a lot, and sooner or later you'll know that I'm telling you the truth."

It took two more days. All of that time Sarah could not keep away from Josh, but she seemed fearful at the same time.

At noon on the second day, they were walking beside the cornfield. They had eaten a quick lunch, and now they were going to work. Josh forgot to limp.

"Josh," she said, "there's nothing wrong with your leg anymore."

"No, and there never has been, Sarah. I pretended to hurt it so I could stay and tell you about us."

Suddenly Sarah turned to him. Her lips were trembling, and her eyes were glistening with tears. "Did you really mean all you've told me, Josh?"

"Yes, I did, Sarah. This is nice, but it's a dream. You need to come back. Both of us have to go back." He had told her about Goél, and now he said, "Goél is depending on us."

Sarah stood absolutely still. The breeze blew her hair, and she looked very young. At last she smiled. It was not a full smile, and her lips still trembled, but she put her hand out timidly. When he took it, she said, "Josh, I'll trust you. I know you couldn't do anything but tell me the truth."

Josh wanted to put his arms around her. Instead he said, "I knew you'd come, Sarah. You couldn't stay here in a dream world. Now, let me tell you what to do . . ."

Sarah awoke to find herself lying on a bed. A sound attracted her attention. She sat up and saw the bodies on two rows of cots. Then she looked down and saw Josh getting to his feet and taking off his headset.

Sarah suddenly realized that she too was wearing a headset. She snapped it off, and then stood as Josh came to his feet. She began to cry. "Josh, you came to get me!"

Josh put his arms around her. "Wash had to come and get me. He's been the only true one. Now, Sarah, we have to get the rest of our group together." When he saw that Wash was still lying beside Reb. He shook his head. "I guess Wash is having a lot of trouble with Reb. You know how stubborn that Southerner is."

"What are we going to do?"

Josh looked at the faces of the Sleepers still trapped in their dream prisons. His face grew tense. "We're going after them and bring them back. And when we get them all here, we'll see about Oliver and his infernal machines!"

12
The Soldier

The jangle of metal, the creaking of leather, and the patter of horses' hooves was on the air as Bob Lee "Reb" Jackson rode down the dusty road. The horse under him was a good strong chestnut, and he was surrounded by riders all in gray. Reb had no eyes for the other cavalrymen, however, for he was watching General Jeb Stuart, who led the troop.

Jeb Stuart was the finest cavalry commander in the Confederacy—many claimed the finest who had ever lived. He rode a coal-black stallion and wore a theatrical uniform. It was ash gray with a cape lined in scarlet and a black slouch hat that had an ostrich plume stuck into the top. He had very light blue eyes and a full, curly auburn beard.

Reb took pride in the battle that they had just fought. He had been in the charge that had broken the enemy's ranks, and he could still feel the thrill as the horse under him strained to keep up with General Stuart. His hand had grown painfully stiff from gripping the hilt of his saber so hard. His throat was raw from the screams that he had uttered along with the others of the troop—the famed Confederate battle cry.

The troop thundered into camp, and Stuart cried, "Dismount!" He threw himself off his horse and tossed the reins to an aide. Reb dismounted and was shocked when General Stuart stepped up and said, "Young man, what's your name?"

"Bob Lee Jackson, sir."

Stuart laughed. "I like to know my new recruits. Those are good names you got. Robert E. Lee and then Stonewall Jackson. Sounds like they all got into your name."

"Yes, sir, they did. I'm proud of those names, General Stuart."

"Well, you did a fine job. I'm gonna expect great things of you, my boy. We've got a hard fight ahead of us, every step of the way, but with men like you I know the Confederacy can win."

Reb felt his legs tremble, for praise from the great Stuart was more than he had anticipated. His fellow cavalrymen pounded him on the shoulders. One of them whispered, "Your first raid, and it looks like you done made your first step toward being a general."

Laughter went around, and Reb blushed. "I don't think I'm quite ready for that, but it was some battle, wasn't it?"

They took care of their horses, and then Reb joined a group that he had grown fond of. He found someone had started a fire, and someone else had found a pig, and soon the smell of roasted meat was sharp on the air.

He sat and listened as older men talked of the great Stuart and the raids he had led them on. One said, "Why, I was there when me and General Stuart rode around the whole Union Army. General McClellan never knowed where we was. That was a fine day for the general."

Reb took his share of the food, ate it hungrily, and washed it down with water from the creek that curled around the section of camp they were in. He finally lay down, hearing the sound of horses stomping and pawing the turf and neighing softly at one another. He knew that guards were posted, and that it was safe to sleep, though the enemy was near. So he closed his eyes, pulled his soft felt hat down over his face, and was instantly asleep.

Something—he never knew what—awaked him sometime during the night. He sensed that it was very late. At first he thought one of his fellow troopers had awakened him, but glancing around he saw that they were all still under their blankets. And the guard had moved to the other end of his post.

Then a figure came out of the darkness and seemed to be searching for something—or someone.

Why, it's a blasted spy! Reb thought at once. Throwing his blanket off, he leaped to his feet and reached out to grab the man. He was shocked to see, however, that is was no more than a boy. Pulling him to the fire, he saw that it was a black boy.

"You been stealin' food, boy?" he demanded sharply, holding the boy's thin arms.

"No, I didn't come to steal anything."

"Well, what are you doing sneaking around here then?"

"I came lookin' to be some help to you."

Well, you got nerve, Reb thought. "Here you come, sneakin' into camp offering to *help* me. Why, you don't even know me."

"Your name's Bob Lee Jackson, but some call you Reb, don't they?"

Reb blinked with surprise. Indeed, he had been called that more than once. "But they call all of us Reb," he said. Then he released the boy. "You get on out of here, boy. You're liable to get hurt."

"Don't some of your men sometimes take their body servants with them when they join the army?"

"Some of the rich men do. They have body servants, but not me. I never had a slave. Don't want one either."

"Never had any slaves? Not any of your family?"

"None of us never had no slaves. We're not fighting this war over slavery. It's over states' rights. We got a right to leave the Union if we want to. Just like we had a right to join it if we wanted to. But I don't want to stand here and argue politics. Now, you get a-movin'. We're going to be pulling out early in the morning."

"Take me with you, please," the black boy said. "I can wash your clothes, and cook your food, and polish your boots, and sharpen your sword. I can do all them things for you. I don't want nothin'—just maybe something to eat."

Reb stared at him. He had, as a matter of fact, a spare horse, which most of the troopers did not. He rubbed his chin thoughtfully. "Well, now, I don't know," he said doubtfully. "Fellows might think I'm kind of stuck-up."

"It don't matter what they think."

"I guess you're right," Reb said with some surprise. "I'll tell you what. You can go along for a while, but when I tell you to go, you got to go. All right?"

"Sure, that's all right. I'll take care of you real good, Mr. Bob Lee Jackson!"

Reb was troubled by the young black boy, Wash, who had come two weeks earlier. At first it had been rather entertaining to have a servant. He had endured a great deal of teasing from his fellow troopers, but he had laughed at them, saying, "You're just jealous 'cause I've got somebody to wait on me."

But as time had gone by, somehow the boy made him nervous. This was difficult to do, for Reb was not a nervous type. He had enough nerve for ten men, as his lieutenant soon found out. He passed the word along to General Stuart.

"If we had five hundred men like that young Jackson, we could take Washington tonight," Stuart had bragged to some of his staff officers. Word had gotten back about this to Reb, and he was proud of it.

Still, there was something about the black boy that *troubled* him. He questioned Wash many times about where he came from, but "Oh, I come from a long way off, Mr. Bob Lee Jackson" was the only answer that he could get out of him.

The thing that really bothered Reb was that he knew he had seen that black boy before. But where? That he could not pin down. He would ask Wash. "Was you ever in Georgia?"

"No, sir."

"How about Alabama?"

"Nope, never in Alabama."

"Mississippi, then. I guess I seen you down in Mississippi. I spent some time down there breakin' some horses for a fella."

"Nope, never was in Mississippi," Wash said.

"Well, I've seen you somewhere."

"I think maybe you have, but it'll have to come to you 'cause I can't say right now."

"Why can't you say?"

"You wouldn't believe it if I told you."

"I probably wouldn't. All you body servants are notorious liars," Reb said half angrily.

They had gone on two more raids. Wash had been left behind, of course, with the cooks and the supply wagons. Reb survived both actions and found himself strangely glad to see the quiet face of the black boy when he got back.

"I thought you might have left while I was gone," he said after the second raid.

"No—waiting for you. You figured out where you seen me yet?"

Reb stared at him. "No, I haven't. I guess I was wrong."

"No, you weren't wrong," Wash said quietly. "It'll come to you."

For days this went on. Reb slept poorly. Dreams came to him—strange dreams about things that he knew could not possibly have happened. He did not share them with anyone, but one day Wash, who was making biscuits, said, "Have you been dreaming about me, Mr. Bob Lee Jackson?"

"How'd you know that?" The sentence was out before Reb could catch it. He stared at the boy with astonishment. "How did you know I dreamed about you?"

"There's lots of things in this world that we can't understand," Wash said. "Ain't that so?"

"Why, I reckon it is. So what about it?"

"I mean, look up at those stars. Look at 'em. There's millions of 'em, and they're always in the same place. What holds them there? Why don't they all fall down? And you know those ducks that came over. How do they know to leave and go south? How do they know to do that?"

"I don't know. They just know, I reckon."

"You know that's not so. Something made 'em that way. This whole world is working, and nobody understands it. But we know that there's something behind it—*somebody* made it. A lot of this world is mighty strange. And those dreams of yours—you don't understand them, do you?"

"No, I don't!" Reb said angrily. "And why would I

dream about you? I dreamed once I was all dressed up in a tin suit. I had some kind of a long spear, and you was ridin' a horse behind me. Crazy dream."

Wash went ahead to tell other experiences the two had had in Camelot.

Reb stared at him, his mouth open.

"You don't know how I know about that dream?"

"No, I don't. Are you a witch of some kind?"

"No, I'm not no witch, no sorcerer, and no magician either. But you see, Reb, those dreams that you keep having—they weren't dreams. They were real."

Reb laughed, at first. "You're as nutty as a pecan orchard!" he said and stalked away.

But time after time Reb would come back and say, "Tell me some more about my dreams." And as Wash told him experiences from life in Nuworld, Reb would grow almost fearful. "There's something wrong with all this," he muttered. "Something real bad about it. I don't know what it is."

One day General Stuart appeared at his tent and said, "We're going into action. Get every man mounted."

Reb said, "I'm glad to get away from you, Wash. You're just driving me crazy. I still think you're some kind of a spook or something."

Wash stood looking after him. "That is one stubborn fellow," he said. "I don't think I'll ever get him to go back to Nuworld. He always loved the South, especially the Confederate Army, even though he never saw it. I guess he's getting his dream, and he ain't going to leave it."

All day he listened to the cannons and the gunfire. The battle was not more than a mile away, and for a long time it seemed unsettled as to who would win.

Finally General Stuart led his men back. Wash saw

Lieutenant Smith, but he could not find Reb. Going to the lieutenant, he said, "Lieutenant Smith, where's Bob Lee Jackson?"

"I'm afraid he got hit. It was bad, Wash. I'm sorry, but he didn't make it."

Wash stared at him and then shook his head. "He made it. I'm going after him." He saddled Reb's spare horse and left the camp, despite Lieutenant Smith's calling, "Come back! Some of those Yankees are still out there."

Wash was not an expert rider, but the horse was not a spirited one. He guided him as best he could, and soon he began to see the dead lying beside the road. Some were in blue uniforms and some in gray. "He can't be dead," he muttered. "He's got to be alive."

Wash got off and checked a body from time to time. Most of them were dead; a few were wounded and struggling to retain life. He saw no signs of Union troops. And then, as he was scurrying around, he heard a voice saying, "Wash . . ."

"Reb!" Wash ran to him.

Reb was lying on his back, struggling to sit up. His right shoulder was bloody and his right side as well.

"Take it easy, Reb," Wash whispered.

"I guess I'm done for," Reb gasped.

"No, you ain't done for. Let me get that horse. We're going to get you to the doctor."

Wash struggled and finally got Reb into the saddle. It was all he could do, for Reb could help very little. "Just hang on, Reb, while I get on behind you. Then I'll hold you on."

They got back to camp with Wash holding the bloody boy in front of him. He slipped off the horse, and troopers came to take Reb's limp body.

"Surgery is right over here. Doctors will get him the best help there is."

General Stuart came. He looked down on the wounded body and shook his head. "Poor boy! Poor boy!"

Reb regained consciousness, then slipped away, many times. For a time he never knew whether he was awake or asleep. He did know that he kept having dreams about dinosaurs, about living under the sea, about men that flew, strange wild dreams, and always, in every dream, the small black boy called Wash was by his side.

Finally, he did awake and saw Wash's face. He licked his lips, and Wash immediately brought water.

"Here now," he said, "hold your head up and sip some of this—not too much now. You can have all you want, but not all at once."

"Where am I?" Reb whispered. His shoulder and side hurt, but he did not allow it to show on his face. "You brought me back?"

"Yes, I did. You're going to be all right, Reb."

Reb reached out, as if he could not believe what he saw, and touched the black face above him. "Wash—"

"Yeah, Reb?"

"You was telling me the truth, wasn't you? About all them things I dream about?"

"Sure was, and I'm going to tell you some more, as you get better."

That was the beginning. It took several days, and Reb listened for long periods without saying a word. It was more than he could understand, but finally the day came when he believed.

"That was real about Camelot. I always wanted to go back there. I remember that now."

"You're going back some day, Reb. It's what you wanted to do more than anything. You were a knight, and there was a lady there that was mighty fond of you."

"I remember," Reb whispered. He looked at the wounded soldiers around him and said, "This isn't real, is it?"

"No, it's just a dream, Reb. Are you ready to go back?"

"I reckon I am. Just tell me how. We better get home, Wash."

13

Another Kind of Cowboy

Reb heard voices, and his eyelids fluttered. Reluctantly, he opened them.

Sarah and Josh stood looking down at him.

"He did it!" Josh exclaimed. "I don't know how, but he got Reb to come back. I bet that wasn't easy."

"Shoot," Reb muttered, "pretty hard to leave bein' a cavalryman with Jeb Stuart and come back to this mess." He swung his feet over the side of the cot and jerked the headset from his temples. Then he reached down and pulled Wash to his feet. Affectionately he said, "Nobody but you could've got me to come back, Wash."

Wash pulled off his own headset and grinned, his white teeth shining against his dark skin. "You just had to come back, Reb. We couldn't get along without you and that fancy ropin' and horse ridin' you do."

Sarah threw her arms around Reb and hugged him tightly. "I know it's hard to come back," she whispered. "It's been hard for all of us—but we had to do it."

Reb grinned and gave her a squeeze. "When I get a pretty little filly like you to give me a hug, I guess I'd come all the way back from Arkansas for that."

Josh slapped Reb on the back, hard. "You son of a gun! I want to hear all about where you were, but not now. What we've got to do right now is get the others back."

Wash took a few steps down the aisle between the

cots. "That's Jake and Dave and Abbey here. You want me to go after one of them, Josh?"

"No, I guess—"

"Well, this is a pretty sight, I must say."

The trio whirled around, and Reb took in a sharp breath.

"Oliver!" Josh gasped. He took a step forward, but Oliver held a strange-looking weapon in his hand—not a gun but a can of some sort. When Josh ignored it, Oliver squirted a vapor that struck the boy right in the face.

Gasping and clawing at his throat, Josh went to his knees, trying desperately to catch his breath.

"Josh!" Sarah screamed and leaped to his side. She held onto him. "What have you done to him, you monster?" she cried, staring at Oliver.

"Nothing permanent. He'll be all right. I have orders from my superior to see that all of you are kept alive for the time being—if possible."

Wash's face grew grim. "And I can guess who your *superior* is. I'd say it's the Dark Lord himself."

"You're a bright boy, Wash." Oliver smiled, but his eyes glittered coldly. "If it weren't for you, this would have gone all right." He held up the can and said, "I ought to give you a double dose. Don't move, or I will."

"What are you up to, Oliver?" Reb demanded. He was ready to throw himself headlong at the man and bring him down. He was big enough and strong enough to do this, but now the can was aimed straight at his face, and he had seen how potent its contents were. "Who are you, anyhow?"

"My real name is Onan."

Josh managed to get a deep breath, although his face was still flushed and he was trembling. "I think I see now. You came out of your hole and got the real Oliver, didn't you?"

"You're a bright boy too, Josh. All of you Sleepers are pretty clever." Onan-Oliver grinned and waved the can slightly toward a cot to his right. "That's Oliver over there. He's having a nice little dream himself. All the others that I was sent to put out of the way, I've got them all now. And I'll soon have you back into your dreams again. Don't move," he warned. "A double dose of this stuff is lethal. I'll try to keep you alive, but it's up to you. Now, all of you lie down on the floor, hands behind your back." Reaching behind him, he pulled forth some fine wire.

When they hesitated, he aimed the can at Sarah's face. "The little lady goes first. She'll be asleep having pleasant dreams soon, or she'll be dead if you don't do as I say. Lie down quick!"

"Lie down, everybody," Josh demanded. "He'll do it."

"Now you're being smart. You first, Joshua."

Josh lay on the floor and put his hands behind him. Keeping his eye on the others, Oliver leaned over and took a turn around Josh's wrist. He was smiling cheerfully and saying, "After all, dreams aren't so bad, are they? Why, I remember—"

Josh flipped over and desperately lashed out with his foot.

"*Ow!*"

His heel caught Oliver in the forehead and knocked him over backward. He dropped the can.

In an instant Oliver was scrambling to his feet.

"Get him!" Wash yelled. "I got the can."

Reb lunged for Oliver, but he tripped over Josh, who was still on the floor.

Oliver whirled and dashed madly out of the room.

"He'll alert the guards," Reb said. "I'll get him."

"No," Josh said, "I'll get him." He shook off the loose wire and leaped to his feet. "You go get Dave, Reb. You've got to bring him back, no matter what you have to do. Sarah, you go get Jake." He was running for the door now and yelled back, "Quick! After Wash and I get Oliver pinned down, we'll go for Abbey, and that'll be all of us."

The sleeping Jake lay on his cot. Sarah quickly moved next to him and attached the extra headset. "Let's do it, Reb," she said, her face touched with strain. "Dave's pretty strong-willed, but you can bring him back."

"Sure, I'll lasso him if I have to," Reb said quickly. He went to Dave's side, put the headset on, and without a moment's hesitation flicked the switch.

The stadium of the Dallas Cowboys was packed. Every available seat was filled, and every spectator was standing up and screaming. Their voices seemed to shake the earth, and they stomped their feet so that the stadium itself trembled as if an earthquake had hit it.

Quarterback Dave Cooper trotted to the huddle. He paused just for a moment and looked up at the stands, a flaming mass of color. His silver helmet caught the sun and he grinned at his teammates. "Well, time for one more play. What'll it be?"

The running back who had broken every record for the Cowboys, said, "Give me the ball, Dave. I can do it."

"You've done it before, Emmitt," Dave said. He considered Smith, but saw that the back's face was tense and that he was limping. "You've carried us all day, and we still got thirty yards to go and have only a few seconds left."

"I can do it, though."

Dave slapped him on the back. "You always think you can do it—and generally you can."

"Let's use the old Hail Mary pass." The fleet split end punched Dave in the side. "Just drop that little bomb right in my hands. I'll catch it and run over anybody that gets in my way."

One by one the Cowboys begged for a chance.

The Super Bowl had been a hard-fought contest. Back and forth the teams had struggled. Now it was the last quarter, and the Cowboys had time for only one more play. A field goal was possible, but they were six points behind.

Dave was weary. He had been sacked four times that afternoon, and now he looked over and saw the monstrous linemen waiting for another chance at him. "They're going to be mean this time," he muttered.

"What'll it be, Dave?" Emmitt asked, still hopeful for a chance.

"The one thing they won't be looking for," Dave Cooper said suddenly.

"What's that?" the right guard asked.

"A quarterback sneak."

"A quarterback sneak?" A groan went up, and the left guard said, "Why, you might make five yards, but as soon as you get away from the line, every one of those secondary backs will be right on you, Dave."

"Then you'll have to get out and run some interference. Come on, let's do it."

The Cowboys broke the huddle and went back to the lineup. Dave stepped up behind the center, wiped his hands on the towel, and stared calmly over at the linebacker, a giant of a man, strong enough to lift a pickup truck. "I'm gonna get you this time, Cooper!" he said through broken teeth. "I'm gonna break you in two!"

"Help yourself, Bob," Dave said cheerfully. He began to call out the signals. The stands had grown strangely quiet. Suddenly the ball slapped into Dave's hands, and the center fired off and knocked two men out of the way, making just enough room for Dave to put his head down and plunge through the line.

Actually it was rather easy because, as he had said, they were not looking for a quarterback sneak. He angled over toward the right corner, but he saw that two of the secondary men were already converging on him and a linebacker was coming to cut him off.

The stands went wild.

Dave sprinted ahead. Then he was glad to see Emmitt Smith coming out of nowhere to pass him and pull out in front. "I'll get one of 'em, Dave," he yelled. Immediately he smashed into the safety, siding him down.

Almost at the same time the left linebacker caught a piece of Dave with his hand. He grasped Dave's jersey, and Dave twisted so that it tore away.

I'm loose! he thought. *Only one man between me and winning the Super Bowl.* But that one man was the best safety in either league. He was fast, strong, and smart.

As Dave approached at full speed, his mind worked like a computer. *He's expecting me to duck left, therefore, I'll duck right. No, that's what he'll think I'm thinking. So I'll duck left anyway. No!*

He had no time left to think for the two were only a few feet apart. The cornerback was waiting for Dave to make his move either right or left, and he was much faster than Dave Cooper, which they both knew.

Suddenly Dave did something that few players had ever done. Instead of trying to dodge, he lowered his head and ran straight into the cornerback. There was a *whoosh* as his shoulders struck the man in his stomach. He felt hands grab at him, and frantically he tore loose. Then, suddenly, he was over the goal line, and pandemonium broke out.

There was time only for the extra point. When it went sailing over the bars, Dave felt himself lifted high in the air. He was carried off the field through what seemed to be insane fans. As he jogged up and down on the shoulders of his teammates, he thought, *Nothing could be better than what I've got right now.*

It took considerable time for the Cowboys to make their way off the field. Then there was the celebration in the locker room. And after that there was to be a celebration at the fanciest ballroom in Dallas. Dave refused a ride, saying, "Nope, I'm gonna drive that new Ferrari of mine. I haven't had a chance to do it much lately."

Dave went to the parking lot and for a moment just looked at the Ferrari. It was the joy of his heart. Owning one had always been the dream of his life, and now it was all his! He opened both wings just for the joy of seeing them fly open, and then slipped behind the wheel.

He was about to close the doors when a man stepped out of the shadows and before Dave could blink was inside the car with him. He had a gun in his hand, and Dave went cold. He knew that there were people in this town who would kill you for a pair of tennis shoes, for a Ferrari, and for the cash he carried. Sudden fear ran through him.

"Drive out of here!"

"You won't get away with this," Dave said hoarsely.

"Well, you won't be around to see me not get away with it." He leveled the gun at Dave's head, and the voice came again in a Southern accent: "Get out of here before I shoot your ears right off, fella."

There was no choice for Dave. He started the powerful engine and asked, "Where are we going?"

"I'll tell you when we get out of here. Now, drive out of this parking lot—and don't try anything funny when we pass the attendant."

That had been in Dave's mind—to make some kind of a signal—but as they approached the entrance, he felt the gun touch his ribs. So when he passed the attendant on duty, all he could do was say, "Good night, George."

"Good night, Mr. Cooper. Congratulations, you was the greatest."

The Ferrari slipped out into the streets, and the Southern voice said, "Turn right and go until I tell you to stop."

It was a long journey for Dave Cooper. He half expected to be shot and his body left in a ditch somewhere outside of Dallas. But no matter how hard he thought, he could not think of how to get out of this mess that he was in.

"How's it feel like to be a Cowboy, a big football hero?"

Dave shook his head. "Look, you can have the car. Just let me out," he said.

"Keep driving." There was a cold threat in the voice, and Dave knew better than to argue.

The trip was confusing. Dave did not know this part of Dallas well, but his captor directed him until they were outside the city. He headed him down a country road to a shabby shack that stood all alone. There was a garage, and the man commanded him brusquely, "Drive into that garage."

Dave pulled the Ferrari inside and sat there feeling sick. "It won't do you any good to kill me," he said. "I can get money for you if that's what you want."

"Get out of the car."

Dave got out and watched as the tall young man shut the ramshackle door, concealing the car. "Get right in there and be careful."

Dave walked out of the garage and to the house. The door was unlocked, but as soon as they were inside the gunman lit a kerosene lantern and shut the door. "Now," he said, "we can get acquainted."

He pulled off the sombrero that had been down over his eyes and said, "Take a good look at me, Dave."

Dave Cooper stared at the young man's blue eyes and fair hair. "I've seen you somewhere before," he said slowly.

"Shore have. Do you remember where?"

"No, I see so many people. Any way, what do you want? You're going to rob me, I guess."

A smile touched the youth's lips. "You football players are pretty tough. I saw you make that last run."

Dave could not think of anything to say to this. "Look, you're letting yourself in for a lot of trouble. You're going to wind up in the penitentiary."

"Nope, I won't do that. What I want is for us to have a nice long talk together. I got some things to say to you, Dave."

Dave was accustomed to fans wanting his attention. *But this guy's a maniac*, he thought with panic. *I've got to get out of here, but he's got the gun.*

"Would you mind pointing that gun the other way?" he said. "It could go off."

The gunman laughed suddenly, and he did not

look, at that moment, dangerous. "It won't go off," he said. "Look." He held it to his own head, and to Dave Cooper's astonishment pulled the trigger. There was a click, and then the young man tossed the gun at him. "Here, look for yourself."

Dave caught the pistol and stared at it. "A toy gun!" he exclaimed.

"I had to get your attention, and real guns can be dangerous."

Dave suddenly felt a streak of anger go over him. "I'm getting out of here, and you're not going with me."

"Well, you can try, but I wish you would listen to me before we have some trouble. All I want is some talk for your own good, Dave."

Dave lunged at him. His fist shot out, aimed straight at the point of his captor's chin, but the chin was not there, and suddenly a blow caught Dave right in the stomach.

"Oooph!" he grunted, and suddenly he could not breathe. He held his stomach, and a blow caught him right in the chest that drove him backwards.

"My name's Reb," the stranger said. "I reckon we're going to get a lot better acquainted, but we got to get this settled. You may be a big, tough football player, but the only way you're going to get out of that door is to beat me to a pulp. So if you got to try it, come on."

What followed was amusing in a way. Dave Cooper was hard and fast and strong. Time and time again he threw himself at Reb, who was taller and faster and stronger. It went on for a long time, until both boys were gasping for breath.

Finally, Dave asked through bruised swollen lips, "What do you want? What's your last name?"

"Reb Jackson. Just a little talk, Dave. That's all. Nothing's going to happen. I promise you that."

Suddenly Dave began to laugh harshly. “Well, it looks like you got the best of the argument. Is there any water around here?”

“I brought some out the other day when I found this place, and some food too. We can make a fire and cook up a little grub.”

Dave Cooper was suddenly intensely curious. “I have seen you before,” he said slowly. He studied the battered face of the tall young man and said, “Well, I’m gonna celebrate. It won’t be what I planned, but I’m starving to death. Let’s fix something to eat, and we can have this talk you want.”

It was Dave’s second day of captivity. At first he had thought he could talk his way out of the situation. He had listened quietly while Reb Jackson had told his wild story. At first, of course, he thought that Reb was insane, but, if so, there seemed to be a method in his madness. What began to convince Dave was the fact that he had dreamed about most of the events that Reb described taking place in Nuworld.

Reb had been calm and patient, but watchful.

Now the sun was setting. The boys sat outside the shack, watching the huge red globe go down, while Reb talked about Goél and Nuworld. “Like I’ve said, Dave, all this is just make-believe. Those ‘dreams’ you’ve been having, they’re what’s real. Goél is real, and Sarah, and most of all for you, I guess, Abbey.”

“Abbey.” This name caught Dave’s attention, and he lifted his head. “What about Abbey?”

“I reckon she’s a goner if you don’t come and help us. We all are. You and Abbey fight a lot, but I reckon you’re going to be pretty close one of these days. As a matter of fact, I think you’re just about half in love with her.”

Despite himself, a picture floated into Dave Cooper's mind. He saw the face of the young girl he had dreamed about constantly. Blonde hair, blue eyes, pretty. He remembered that in the dreams he would get aggravated with her for acting foolishly sometimes, but then there were other dreams in which the sweetness of the girl just almost overwhelmed him.

Reb said quickly, "It's up to you, Dave. You don't *have* to come back. I can't make you. Nobody can make you. Sooner or later you'll wear me out here, and you can go back to being a big football hero. You can drive fancy cars and all that, but just remember, Dave, it's not real."

All night long, after the two went to bed, Dave thought of what Reb had said. His mind was in turmoil, but again and again he heard those words *It's not real.*

When the sun came up, the boys ate the last of the supplies, then Reb said, "Well, I can't hold you here forever. You know that, Dave. Sooner or later a man's got to stand for what's right. I've told you what's right. Now what are you going to do?"

Dave Cooper had already made his decision. He said slowly, "I don't know, Reb. I think I'm crazy, and I think you're crazy. If all this is a dream, it's been a lot of fun, but a man can't spend his life dreaming, can he?"

"No, he can't. Does that mean you're going back?"

Dave Cooper, quarterback of the Dallas Cowboys —at least in his dreams—nodded slowly. "I guess it does, Reb. Let's get back and do what has to be done."

14

Ensign Jake Garfield

"Would you like to join me in the lounge after you're off duty, Ensign Garfield?"

Jake Garfield, of the spaceship *Avenger*, turned quickly.

Commander Ceri Tirion stood watching him, her lips turned upward in a welcoming smile. Her enormous eyes always seemed to hold an invitation, and her long, glossy black hair was exactly the shade that Jake had always liked.

"Why, I'd be glad to, Commander." Jake always felt bashful and ill at ease with this superior officer.

Her smile widened. "I'll be waiting for you."

"Ensign Garfield!"

Jake whirled the other direction and found an extremely tall man with a pair of intense eyes fixed upon him. "Yes, sir, Captain Drystan."

Hugo Drystan, commanding officer of the *Avenger*, was not a man one could ignore. Jake had admired him from afar, and now, as communications officer on the *Avenger*, he was anxious to please his new chief.

"We will be leaving this galaxy in exactly seven minutes, Ensign. You will take the helm."

"Me, sir?"

Drystan's eyes narrowed. "That's what you've come aboard for—to learn how to command a spaceship of the Imperial Fleet. Have you changed your mind?"

"Oh, no, sir," Jake said quickly. "I appreciate the opportunity to serve under you."

Drystan smiled slightly. “It’s a little bit frightening being a young ensign. I remember when I was one myself in the Dark Ages. Do your duty, and we will see how it goes.”

Nervously, Jake sat in the chair that the captain had vacated. He was aware of the sinister Lieutenant Zeno, the *Avenger*’s chief gunner, glaring at him. It made him nervous, and he tried to ignore Zeno’s smoldering eyes.

He handled the starship acceptably, however, and gave a sigh of satisfaction when Captain Drystan finally said, “You’re relieved. Good job, Ensign Garfield.”

Jake left the bridge. As he walked down an outside corridor toward the lounge, he was surprised to find Lieutenant Zeno beside him. He always felt like a child beside the huge man. Clearing his throat, he said, “It’s good to serve on the *Avenger*, Lieutenant Zeno.”

“I would advise you not to get too friendly with Commander Tirion.”

Jake stopped, surprised by Zeno’s harsh remark. “Why do you say that, Lieutenant?”

“You’re not her kind.” There was an almost cruel gleam in the man’s eyes.

Jake started to reply when suddenly the loudspeaker said, “Ensign Garfield, report to the bridge at once.”

Holding up his wrist radio, Jake said quickly, “Yes, sir!” He left Zeno, glad to be out from under the baleful scrutiny of the man’s brooding eyes.

When he arrived back at the bridge, Captain Drystan turned to him. “We have a problem, Ensign. An alien has just been scanned aboard ship. Take care of him. Be certain that he is not free to roam the ship. I will see him when I am free from my duties here.”

“Yes, sir.”

Jake took the elevator down to the master macroscanner's station. The dark-haired officer gave him an odd smile. "Well, there's your alien, Ensign. Doesn't look too dangerous, I'd say."

Some young women stood just to the left of the platform where crew members and others were beamed out and returned through a transcarrier.

Stepping forward, he said, "What's your name?"

"My name is Sarah."

"Sarah?" The name had a familiar ring, and Jake's forehead wrinkled. "What is your business aboard the *Avenger?*"

"I came to find you, Jake."

The lieutenant who operated the macroscanner could not suppress a slight laugh.

But Jake asked, "What do you mean, you've come to find me?"

"I've come such a long way, Jake," Sarah said. She moved closer to him, put her hand on his chest. "Don't you remember me at all?"

Lieutenant Zeno suddenly entered and towered over both of them. "Is this the alien?" he demanded.

"Why, yes, Lieutenant, but—"

"I will take charge of her."

"But Captain Drystan ordered me—"

Zeno gave Jake a killing look, then turned and walked stiffly away.

"What's the matter with him? Why is he so angry?" Sarah asked.

Jake didn't know how to answer that. He knew that Lieutenant Zeno was in love with Ceri Tirion, and it had occurred to him that the man was jealous. "Never mind that," he said quickly. "Come with me. I'll see that you have proper quarters until Captain Drystan can speak with you."

As he began to lead her out of the room, the macroscanner operator turned to his assistant. "Well," he said, with raised eyebrows. "Sarah, is it? Pretty little thing, and she knows Ensign Garfield. Now, that is interesting . . ."

Jake thought it was interesting too, but it troubled him. He strode quickly down the corridor until he came to a door that opened as he approached it. Stepping inside, he waited for the girl and said, "These will be your quarters."

He turned to leave, but she said, "Please, Jake, let me talk with you awhile."

"How do you know my name?" Jake said curiously. He studied her features carefully. She was small, graceful, had large brown eyes and very black hair. She was wearing a strange costume, a simple dress, and he tried to identify it. "I've seen someone dressed like that before. Perhaps I saw a picture in a book?"

"It comes from a long time ago. How long have you been on this spaceship?"

"Not too long," Jake said. "Why do you keep asking about me—and why do you keep looking at me in such a strange way?"

"Jake, we've known each other in another time and in another place." Sarah came close and put her hand on his arm. She whispered, "We were friends in another life."

"What are you talking about?" Jake asked. "You look familiar, but what's this about another life?"

Sarah hesitated, then said, "I don't know any way, Jake, to get at this thing except just to tell you the truth." She waved her hand around the room. "All of this is just a dream. You're *dreaming* that you're on a spaceship. Back home you always liked those old TV programs and the science-fiction movies."

"What do you mean? I don't know what you're talking about."

"There *is* no *Avenger*. I know that's hard for you to believe." She reached out and tapped the bulkhead. "See. It makes a noise, but that's the way dreams are. Sit down, Jake, and let me tell you who I am and who you are."

Jake suddenly clamped his lips together. "I *know* who I am. I'm Ensign Jake Garfield of the spaceship *Avenger*. What I *don't* know is who you are and why you are lying to me like this."

At that moment the door opened, and three people entered: Captain Drystan, Commander Tirion, and Lieutenant Zeno.

"Oh, Captain," Jake said, stepping back. "This young lady says her name is Sarah."

"Has she told you why she has come aboard my ship?" Drystan asked, looking at Sarah suspiciously.

Jake's face flushed. "Well, sir, she says she's come to find me."

Drystan smiled slightly. "I didn't know you were such an attractive fellow that beautiful young ladies would come into space seeking you." He must have seen Jake's confusion. He turned to Ceri Tirion. "What do you make of this, Commander?"

Ceri Tirion fixed her enormous dark eyes on Sarah. She studied her carefully, and the room grew very quiet. Finally she said, "I think the girl is telling the truth. There's no evil in her. She has truly come on board seeking Ensign Garfield."

Zeno growled, "And what would you want with an officer of the Imperial Space Fleet?"

Sarah said, "You wouldn't believe me if I told you."

Ceri Tirion put an arm around her. "I might believe

you, Sarah. Why don't you come with me to my quarters? We can talk there."

Drystan nodded slightly, and the two women left.

Zeno said immediately, "She's obviously a spy of some sort, Captain." He turned to glare at Jake. "And you know her, you say?"

"No, I don't. She claims to know *me*," Jake blurted.

"Well, Commander Tirion will sort it all out, I'm sure," Drystan said. "After she has finished with her examination, perhaps you'll know a little more about why this woman has come through deep space to seek you out."

Jake watched the captain and Zeno leave, then followed them outside. They seemed to have forgotten him, however, and he wandered back to his own quarters. When he was inside, he called forth a glass of pink lemonade, which was created merely by the sound of his voice. It was a drink that he alone on the *Avenger* loved. He went over and looked out the space window at the millions of stars that sailed by, turning into fine points of light as the *Avenger* flashed past them at light speed. He never tired of watching the heavens.

Finally he went back and lay down on his bed. "Sarah . . ." he said. For a while he thought of the girl and at last dropped off into sleep.

Sarah almost despaired of ever convincing Jake that everything about him was merely an illusion. For more than a week she had seen him every day, but nothing changed his mind. He would sit and stare at her as she recounted adventure after adventure that the two had shared in Nuworld. His eyes would grow thoughtful, but there was a stubborn line through his lips, and he would either say nothing or else shake his head and insist, "*Those* are dreams you are talking about. *This*—" he would knock on the floor or tap the ceiling "—this is reality, Sarah."

Commander Tirion had several interviews with Sarah, then reported the result of them to Drystan. "Captain," she said, "I am very puzzled."

They were in his cabin, sipping cool fruit drinks, and Drystan held his up to the light. "This is good," he said, then his attention came back. "I've heard the girl's story. All about how earth was blown up in a nuclear war, and seven children were saved, coming out years later into a world blasted by the holocaust." He shook his head. "She tells the story well enough. She has a remarkable imagination. I can almost see some of those things she talks about."

"What's your opinion of her, sir?"

Drystan's eyebrows arched. "My opinion? She seems to be a sweet young girl. But what's more important, Commander, is what you, a woman, think of her?"

Ceri Tirion leaned back and ran a hand over her dark hair. "I'm very puzzled. There's no evil in her, of that I am sure, and she's totally convinced that what she says is true. She's not deliberately lying about these things."

"Are you telling me she's insane?"

"No, I didn't say that."

"Men who claim to be Napoleon Bonaparte, no matter how sincere they are, are usually considered mentally aberrant."

"This girl has none of those signs of insanity. And she really believes what she's saying." The commander took a sip of juice, licked her lips, and then smiled. "Wouldn't it be odd if she were telling the truth? If all of this *is* a dream."

Drystan did not answer. He simply shook his head.

"She's got Ensign Garfield half convinced, I think. He pretends to be resisting her story, but I can tell that she's having an influence on him. Do you think so?"

"She's very convincing indeed, and Ensign Garfield is very young. I've learned that he has had dreams of the very things that she's told him about. Now, he's beginning to wonder if the dreams are the reality and we are the illusion. It will be interesting—" she smiled again— "to find out which is the truth."

Jake was in an agony of indecision. He had tried time and time again to trap Sarah, but she always told her stories exactly the same way, and the rub of it all was that Jake found himself seeming to remember the very things she talked about. The more she told him about Nuworld and Josh, and Wash, and all of the other Sleepers, the more real it all became.

But he remained adamant. He growled more than once, "She's not going to get me away from here. No, she's crazy, and that's all there is to it."

The middle of the second week of Sarah's visit to the *Avenger*, she had an idea. It came to her rather uncertainly at first and then grew stronger. Finally, when she and Jake were again talking in her quarters, she said, "Jake, I want you to do something."

"I'll bet you do." Jake grinned. "You want me to go back and get eaten up by one of those horrible creatures. That's what's going to happen to everybody back in—what do you call it?—Nuworld?"

"You're trying to make fun of me, Jake, but there's one thing you won't try." Sarah's eyes were challenging, and when he looked at her she said, "Let's go down to the Viewing Room."

"You want to play *games* at a time like this?"

"Yes, I do. Will you take me there?"

"If you say so. I've always liked the Viewing Room."

They went down into the level of the ship where the Viewing Room was installed. It was a large room that, through the miracles of science, could be transformed into anything the viewer wished. He could be an explorer in Africa, and the room would suddenly be a jungle, with tigers, lions, and screaming monkeys. It could be a desert with camels and miles of burning sand.

Jake said, "Well, how should we program it?"

"I want to program it for the time that we flew on the backs of eagles, far above the deserts."

Jake stared at her. Sweat broke out on his forehead, but he tried to appear casual. "Anything you say, Sarah." He made the necessary adjustments, and . . .

Suddenly Jake found himself in a different world. It was a world of blue sky and white clouds and golden sun, and then he realized that his legs were astride a huge, feathered neck. Leaning forward, he saw that the head at the end of that neck was the head of a magnificent eagle. He shut his eyes, refusing to look further.

"Look down, Jake. Look down. There are the other Sleepers. Do you see?"

Jake heard Sarah's voice, and, swallowing hard, he straightened up and forced himself to open his eyes. The eagle's mighty pinions, fully thirty feet across, were beating the air. Turning to his right, he saw Sarah astride an enormous bird like the one he rode. She was laughing, and her hair was flying. "Look, Jake. There they are down there."

Jake looked downward and saw tiny figures. His eagle suddenly wheeled, and his stomach wheeled also. But as the eagles flew closer to the ground, he found that he recognized the young people below.

"That's Josh, and that's Reb Jackson," he murmured, "and Dave Cooper, and Abbey Roberts, and there's Wash. *I know them all.*"

He gasped as his eagle suddenly beat its wings harder and mounted upward toward the sun.

Sarah called out, "Do you believe now, Jake?"

Jake looked back down at the young people, stared at them hard, then turned away. Sarah was looking at him with pleading in her eyes and then reached out a hand toward him. "Do you believe now, Jake?"

And Jake Garfield suddenly knew that this experience had actually happened. He knew that Sarah had been telling the truth. "Yes," he called out, "I believe."

And then he found they were back in the Viewing Room.

After Jake and Sarah had sat in silence for a moment, she took his hand. "It's hard to give up your dreams, isn't it, Jake?"

"Yes, it is. Did you have to give up a dream, too, Sarah?"

"All of us had to give up dreams. All except Wash. He's the only one who didn't get fooled. And nobody really got to 'go home.' Oliver deceived us. Are you ready to go back to Nuworld, Jake?"

"Yes, I'm ready now, Sarah."

15
The Ball

Dave looked down at his clothes and saw that he was indeed in a dream. He was not yet quite sure what dream Abbey had chosen, but the costume he had on seemed vaguely familiar. He wore a pair of fawn-colored trousers, a multicolored waistcoat, a snow-white shirt with ruffled front, a black tie, and a cropped coat that came to his knees. He pulled off his hat and saw that it was light tan with a sweeping, broad brim and a low crown. Putting it back on and settling it at an angle, he muttered, "I'm all dressed up for something—but I don't know what."

Looking about, he saw that he stood in front of one of the most magnificent homes that he had ever seen. It sat well back from the road, was surrounded by enormous oak trees, and looked very familiar. It was a large plantation house, gleaming white. The grassy grounds were manicured to an even height. "I've seen that place before somewhere," Dave muttered. He began drifting toward it.

"Where *is* this place? It looks so familiar . . ."

He came closer and saw black servants, men and women, moving about and serving a large crowd that had gathered on the lawn. "It's back in the old South—I recognize that much. Abbey always liked stories like that. Well, I look the part. I'll just go join the party."

Large tables draped with white cloths were set up on the green grass in front of the house. Cut crystal caught the reflection of the sun and glittered like diamonds. Men were sipping frosty-looking drinks out of tall, thin glasses with green sprigs on top. "Those must be mint juleps. I've read about them," Dave said, "but I've never actually seen one."

He moved among the crowd, listening to the soft murmur of Southern voices, and then suddenly he accidentally bumped into someone.

"Oh, sorry," he said, turning around.

"That's all right. My fault." The speaker was a tall, strongly built man with black hair and a black mustache neatly clipped. He had a ruggedly handsome face and was dressed much as Dave himself was. "I don't believe I know you, sir."

"I'm Dave Cooper, sir." Dave added the "sir," feeling that the man had the right touch of language.

"Captain Breck Stewart."

Breck Stewart! Dave gasped. The hero in Abbey's favorite TV program. *Now she must be right in the middle of it!*

"Captain Stewart," he said and shook the strong hand of the handsome man in front of him. "Are you back from having run the blockade?" In the television series, Stewart was a ship owner who ran a blockade during the Civil War, bringing war supplies past the federal gunships.

"Yes, we had a very successful cruise this last time."

"I'm glad to hear it. I'm sure your cargo was welcomed here in the Confederacy."

"They need everything." Stewart seemed to smile without moving his lips. "I suppose you've come to call on one of the beautiful ladies of the house."

"Well," Dave said, "I won't be calling on Miss Elizabeth Brady. I understand you're courting her, Captain Stewart."

Stewart looked at him with surprise. "Why, no. Go right ahead and court Miss Elizabeth. She's a beautiful young lady."

Dave was confused, "You haven't come calling on Elizabeth Brady? But I thought—"

"No, I'm very interested in her cousin."

"Her cousin? I don't believe I've met her."

"Then you must. She's the toast of the Confederacy. Why, there she is now. Come along. I'll introduce you, but—" Stewart grinned and added jovially "—no competition. I don't want to have to fight another duel."

Somehow Dave knew, before he looked up at the young lady, what he would see, and he did.

Breck Stewart said, "Miss Abbey Roberts, may I present to you Mr. Dave Cooper. He's come courting, but I've given him stern warning he's to leave you to my tender mercy."

"Why, Captain Stewart, how dare you say such a thing." Abbey was wearing a beautiful orchid-color dress over a full set of hoops. She wore a straw hat over her blonde hair, and she looked beautiful.

"I'm happy to make your acquaintance, Miss Roberts," Dave said formally.

"Perhaps I can introduce you to some of the other young ladies."

"Well, despite Captain Stewart's warnings, I'd much rather talk with you."

A dangerous glint came into Breck Stewart's eyes. He stared hard at Dave, then turned and walked away without another word.

"Really, Mr. Cooper, you must be careful! Captain Stewart's already shot more than one man in a duel."

"I know he has. I'm surprised he's not interested in your cousin Elizabeth."

"Oh, he *was* interested in her," Abbey said lightly,

and her eyes gleamed. "But then he seemed to prefer my company."

"How does Elizabeth like that?" He knew that Elizabeth, in the TV series, was a possessive woman.

"Oh, she doesn't care anything about Breck Stewart, but I do." Abbey put her hand over her mouth, and her eyes flew wide. "Well, I'll declare. Here I am telling you, a total stranger, all these things."

"I won't breathe a word of it to a soul, Miss Abbey," he said. "Could I get you some refreshment?"

"Why, that would be very nice." Abbey's eyes fluttered toward Stewart, who had stationed himself across the lawn and was watching her with a slight smile. "But you must be careful. Captain Stewart's very jealous."

Dave said, "I will be very careful, Miss Abbey." But he thought, *One good thing about this is that, as long as this is a dream, if Stewart shoots me I won't really be dead. It makes it easy for a fellow to be brave.*

As the party progressed, it became more and more obvious that Abbey was completely submerged in the world of her TV people. Dave had not the foggiest idea of how to help her.

He moved among the crowd, staying always close to her, seeing Elizabeth and her sisters, listening as the men talked about the war, and always thinking, *How can I get Abbey out of this? She always loved romantic stories on TV shows, and now she's the star of one.*

Despair came over him. He knew that it would take every ounce of ingenuity he could find to extract Abbey Roberts from her dream world.

He managed to finagle an invitation from Elizabeth Brady herself to come back. She was a beautiful girl, selfish to the core, exactly as she was in the TV show. She said, "In fact, you ought to stay for a few days as our house guest. I noticed that you're interested in my cousin, Miss Abbey."

"Yes, I am," Dave said boldly. "Captain Breck Stewart, I believe, is interested also."

"He is a wicked man," Elizabeth said. "I would have nothing to do with him, and I've warned Abbey to do the same. Be careful—if you make Captain Stewart jealous, he might shoot you."

"Well, I might shoot him," Dave said jokingly.

That thought seemed to intrigue Elizabeth Brady. "Why, yes, you must stay," she said. "We have plenty of room. I'll see that you have a horse to ride." She leaned closer, and Dave could smell her lavender perfume. "I'll help you win Miss Abbey. Won't that make Captain Stewart mad?"

"I expect it would," Dave said, "but I do appreciate all the help you can give me, Miss Elizabeth."

Elizabeth was true to her word. Dave stayed on at the Brady plantation for several weeks. As happens in dreams, no one seemed to question his presence there. Mr. Brady liked him, and he often went hunting with the older man.

But it was Abbey who got most of his attention. He discovered that she delighted in the world of the South. Dave had read some history. He knew that period had been a time of a few very rich planters and huge numbers of very poor farmers. These planters weren't the real South, but they were the most colorful. They had the money, and the fine houses, and the fine horses. He tried to explain this to Abbey but soon gave up. The world of the rich planters, their handsome sons, their hot-blooded horses, their midnight cake bakes all pleased her immensely.

Breck Stewart frequently visited the plantation.

More than once his eyes had grown cold when he saw Dave and Abbey together. Abbey, of course, would shiver and warn Dave, "You must be careful. He's a very dangerous man."

"And very attractive," Dave suggested.

"Yes, of course, he is that." Abbey touched his arm. "So are you, David. I've never known anyone finer."

The crisis came unexpectedly. Stewart evidently had been drinking. He appeared suddenly in the middle of a party where Dave and Abbey were laughing with some other young people. Abbey saw him first, and her eyes flew open wide. "Dave," she whispered, "he's coming to challenge you. Don't do it."

Dave turned to face the man who suddenly stood over him. "Yes, Captain Stewart?" he asked. "Can I do something for you?"

Without warning, Stewart slapped Dave across the face. "You can get out and run like a cur, or you can meet me and we'll have this out like men."

A cry went up from those around them, but not a very loud one. Dueling was the custom in the South. And Dave well knew that a man who refused to avenge an insult such as he had received would be scorned by everyone. He glanced quickly around and then eyed Breck Stewart. "I'll meet anywhere you say, Captain."

"At dusk then. At the old barn where the roads cross." Stewart walked away.

"You can't do it, Dave," Abbey whispered. "You just can't."

"I've got to. You saw what he did. You heard what he said." Dave was thinking, *Maybe this will shake her up. It's a duel, and I don't believe in such things, but after all, this is just her dream.*

Word spread all over the plantation, and Dave

received much advice on how to duel. As his counselors talked, their eyes glittered with excitement, and he knew they were thinking, *He may be dead by the time it's dark!*

He went to his room, put on a fine suit, and left the house at four o'clock. He rode to the crossroads where he found Stewart waiting. "I'm sorry to be late," he said, stepping off the horse.

"Go home, boy," Stewart said. "Get away from this place. No sense dying for a girl."

"Well, you're ready to die for one," Dave challenged.

"No, I'm not. Besides, you're just a boy. Have you ever fought a duel before?"

Dave thought of some of the duels he had endured with dreadful beings back in Nuworld. "I've fought my share," he said firmly.

Stewart's eyes narrowed. "Well," he said, "here are two pistols. Take your pick."

Dave chose one pistol, and Breck Stewart took the other. "Will you load them, or shall I?"

"You do the loading, Captain Stewart."

"Very well." Stewart loaded the dueling pistols expertly and held them both out. "Again, take your pick."

Dave took the one nearest him. "This one will do."

"Very well. We don't have any seconds, so we'll stand back to back. You count off ten paces. When you have the count of ten, I'll turn and you turn, and we'll fire at will."

"Very well," Dave said. "Shall we begin?" He noticed a buggy approaching, a black servant driving wildly, whipping the horses—and a girl in the back. But he said, "I'm ready."

He turned and felt Stewart touch him as they

stood back to back. Holding up his pistol, he said, "One," and took a step. "Two," another step. "Three, four." He counted slowly, taking one step each time. "Six, seven, eight—"

The sound of wheels and horses' hooves thundered behind him.

"Wait! Oh, wait!" Stewart shouted.

Confused, Dave turned to see Abbey Roberts standing between him and Captain Stewart.

A look of chagrin came over the captain's face. He said bitterly, "It's hard to fight a duel over you, Abbey, when you're standing in the way. I'd have to shoot through you to kill him. Well, go ahead and take him then, if you think that much of him." He turned, mounted his horse, and rode away without even retrieving his other dueling pistol.

"Thanks, Abbey," Dave said. "I wouldn't have had much chance with him."

"Dave, I don't know why I did it."

"I do. Come, sit over here, Abbey. I've got some things to tell you—"

For a long time Abbey sat on the grass and listened as Dave spoke earnestly and eloquently. They finally got into the buggy and went back to the plantation.

When she got down and started for the house, Dave turned her around. "I guess I might as well tell you this, Abbey. We had some fights in those days, but I grew to love you in Nuworld, and I love you now more than ever. Come back with me."

Abbey must have felt totally confused, as the other Sleepers had been in the middle of their dreams. Dave saw this. "I told you how hard it was for me. I know it'll be hard for you. I know what will happen, though. Tonight you'll dream of the way it was, you and me, and you'll come back with me. I'll wait over there." He looked up and saw the moon beginning to rise. "Come when you're ready to go, Abbey."

The moon was a huge silver medallion high in the sky when Abbey came quietly out of the house. The green grass was soft under her feet. The summer air was warm. She wore a simple blue dress, and the wind stirred her hair, framing her face.

When she came up to Dave, she smiled, but there were tears in her eyes, "Do you really love me, Dave?"

"Yes."

"Then I'm ready. Let's go back."

16
Goél Speaks

Back in Nuworld, once his missing servants were freed from their dreams, Goél gathered the Seven Sleepers into one small, cramped room. "It is all over, then?" he asked. "The nightmare of the Dream Maker?"

"Yes, Goél," Josh said. Wash thought he looked somewhat embarrassed. "It was all my fault. I should have known that the man wasn't Oliver."

"It wasn't your fault, Josh," Sarah said quickly. "How could you have known? He *said* the right thing."

The false Oliver had, indeed, captured the true one. He'd confessed to intercepting Goél's helper and taking his place after forcing him to reveal the password. Angry with the Dark Lord for failing him, Onan-Oliver smashed the Dream Maker, thus releasing all Goél's missing servants. And now the inventor was held captive in the same prison where he had once held all the others.

"Do not blame yourself, my son," Goél said. "You were faithful in the end." Looking around, he smiled. "You all were. I am pleased."

"What happens now, Goél?" Wash asked. "You said before we began this mission that the last battle would be soon."

"Yes, Wash. It will be soon. I will not name dates or times, but you must hold yourselves in readiness. The Dark Lord has summoned all the hosts of his evil servants. They are foul, but powerful."

A silence fell over the room. Wash knew that

everyone wanted to ask about the battle, but no one dared. Finally, he said, "Are there more of them than there are of us?"

"There are always more with us than with them."

Wash held himself straighter, and nodded almost fiercely. "Then let them come. As long as you are with us, Goél, we can whip 'em."

"Sure we can," Reb said, yanking his hat off and slapping it against his thigh. His light blue eyes gleamed. "When does the fracas start?"

Goél laughed. "I would not call such a titanic battle as we face a *fracas*. However, I'm glad to see that you're ready for whatever comes, Robert." He was the only one who ever called Reb "Robert," and now he gazed fondly at the gangling young man.

Then Goél looked about at each of them. "When you were dreaming, you had all that you had always longed for—and yet you chose to come back to danger, death, pain." He was silent then, but Wash felt the glow of his approval. "All seven of you. I have chosen my servants well." He gathered his robe about him and began to speak of what was to come. He ended by saying simply, "Keep yourselves available. When the call for battle comes, you must move quickly. Now, I must go. Remember, the House of Goél will be filled!"

And then he was gone, vanishing out of their sight.

Wash said, "How does he *do* that?"

"I guess he can do anything he wants to," Josh said. "And now we'll just have to wait."

"We've done a lot of that. I just don't care to do much *dreaming* for a while," Dave said, laughing shortly.

"I don't either," Jake said. "It was fun being on a starship like I always wanted to be, but it wasn't real."

"No, it wasn't," Josh said. He smiled at Sarah.

"Would you like to go back to your dream again, Sarah?"

"No, that's over. It was never really what I wanted. I don't think we can hide behind our dreams. That would be foolish."

He said, "Come along, and you can tell me about it. Time to go for a walk. I want to hear more about what you liked about me that made you come all the way back."

The two left, laughing, and then abruptly Dave said, "I guess there's room for two more out there, Abbey. Want to take a walk in the moonlight?"

Abbey looked up. "Did you mean what you said—back in that dream, Dave?"

He looked around with some embarrassment, then straightened up. "Sure, I meant it. Come on, Abbey, let's get away from these yahoos."

When both couples were gone, Reb and Jake and Wash looked at each other.

There was amusement in Reb's eyes. "Sure is funny how guys get all interested in girls. Mostly they get their feet tangled up. I'm glad I don't have that to worry about."

"I guess it's all right for them," Wash said, going to the door and watching the two couples fade away into the darkness. Then he turned to Jake. "What are we going to do now?"

Jake said, "I don't know. What about you, Reb? You got any ideas?"

"Let's go trot-lining. I'd like to catch a big old catfish. One as long as you are, Jake."

Jake's eyes lighted up. "That would be good. Catfish, and hush puppies, and fried onion rings. Let's do it!"

All three headed for the river, where they kept a

small boat. Soon they were skimming over the surface of the water, the sound of their laughter carrying far.

Overhead the silver moon beamed down on the couples walking along the river.

Josh listened with a smile as the boys broke the silence of the night with their yelling. He said, "They're sure having fun."

"Yes, they are, and so am I."

Josh looked down at Sarah and said quietly, "I guess we don't have to dream. We've got the real thing."

"Yes, we have." She moved closer, and his arm crept around her. They wandered on down the riverbank, walking slowly and speaking quietly.

Farther downstream, Dave said with a smile, "I sure did like to dress up and play a Southern gentleman. Those were good times, weren't they?"

"I don't think times were ever really like they were in that TV series."

"You don't? I thought you liked all that, Abbey." He looked down at her face and thought again how pretty she was. He took her hand. "You always gave me the impression you'd like to go back and live in the old South."

"Not really," Abbey said. Then she stopped walking and looked up at him. "This time is good enough for me—and this place."

"Well, if you like me better than Breck Stewart, I guess we've got something going." He pulled her close and held her for a moment, whispering, "You're prettier than Elizabeth Brady!"

The Seven Sleepers Series includes:

- Flight of the Eagles—#1
- The Gates of Neptune—#2
- The Sword of Camelot—#3
- The Caves That Time Forgot—#4
- Winged Raiders of the Desert—#5
- Empress of the Underworld—#6
- Voyage of the Dolphin—#7
- Attack of the Amazons—#8
- Escape with the Dream Maker—#9

Moody Press, a ministry of the Moody Bible Institute,
is designed for education, evangelization, and edification.
If we may assist you in knowing more about Christ
and the Christian life, please write us without obligation:
Moody Press, c/o MLM, Chicago, Illinois 60610.